TIGER KITTENS

TIGER KITTENS

ALBERT ZUCKERMAN

PUBLISHED FOR THE CRIME CLUB BY
DOUBLEDAY & COMPANY, INC.
GARDEN CITY, NEW YORK
1973

All of the characters in this book
are fictitious, and any resemblance
to actual persons, living or dead,
is purely coincidental.

First Edition

ISBN: 0-385-02440-1
Library of Congress Catalog Card Number: 72–84958
Copyright © 1973 by Albert Zuckerman
All Rights Reserved
Printed in the United States of America

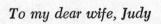

To my dear wife, Judy

TIGER KITTENS

CHAPTER 1

Sliding her hand forward along the railing, then clutching it tightly so she could lower herself lightly, silently, tiptoeing step by step, Daphne was counting. Three more, two more, one more, and that would be the end. Then maybe her heart would stop pounding so hard, and her stomach pain would go away. Because then she'd know if Daddy really was inside one of those windows —if he was all busy doing a secret mission, so he *couldn't* have answered the doorbell, or if this whole thing was only a wild-goose chase, and Mom had sent her over here just to get her out of the house so she wouldn't be a nuisance.

At least half a dozen people saw the dark-haired little girl in the striped green dress working her way down the fire escape. There was no direct sun in this back canyon between two rows of dilapidated apartment houses. But it was a pleasantly hazy spring afternoon, and for the elderly inhabitants who sat quietly at their windows, this view of clotheslines to which bright jerseys might be pinned, of house plants which might get watered, rugs beaten, children called, meant contact with the living. Normally, anyone seen creeping down a fire escape would have been suspect, the police promptly called.

There'd been too many burglaries. It was completely crazy. But still, they'd lived too long to grow alarmed by a child who looked no more than ten, probably less, and wore bows in her hair.

Daphne crouched, knelt and then stretched out prone. She didn't mind the metal slats pressing into her a little, but why did they have to be so dirty? Why did everything you touched in New York have to get you so black and sooty? Her dress, with all the rips it had now, was probably ruined too. Mom would hit her. But maybe not, if she could sneak straight into her room, slip it off, then later bundle it into the incinerator. Sure, she could say it got lost at the cleaner's.

Her heart was getting so loud, almost like the bass drum in her old music class. Bomp-bomp, bomp-bomp. Bomp—her head hit the brick. Had anyone heard? She waited, holding her breath. Slowly she was raising her hand, feeling brick, brick, then wood. Yes, the sill. Something crumbled. Its paint was cracking. Grimy on one side, the little chip was smooth and white on the other.

She pulled her knees in under her, and inched her head up, higher, higher . . .

Shut, the window was shut.

Then a teeny bit higher still.

Crumb! The shade was down too, all the way to the bottom. She felt like closing her eyes and sleeping.

But—but there was another window. Fire escapes have two windows, always. Never three, though. And if Daddy was here, it would have to be open. Because otherwise it would be too hot inside. Unless maybe he had to keep it closed for security, so enemy agents couldn't look in with telescopic lenses. But she wasn't any enemy.

Snail-like, she arched up her rear, pivoted, and crawled closely along the scratchy bricks. Bomp-bomp, bomp-bomp. Again she raised her head.

Open, it was open! A nice thick black crack. She couldn't really see anything, but maybe she'd be able to hear, and then maybe her eyes would get accustomed, and she *would* be able to see.

After a long minute, one black thing took the shape of a dresser, then next to it a table, with a typewriter on it, and a briefcase. The thing near the table should have been a chair, and then she realized it was. It looked so queer, though, because there was stuff piled over it, clothes probably. But where was Daddy? And weren't there going to be any other agents?

She heard a noise. Bathroom flush sounds, a faucet on and then off, a door opening, soft footsteps. Was someone not wearing shoes? She saw a leg, bare skin, and then it stayed bare, going all the way up to—breasts, long hair— a woman. Who? Why was she naked?

"So? Still 'annoyed' I surprised you?"

The voice sounded nice, like she could have a dimple and a smile.

"Guess?"

A man? Yes, it was. And that briefcase. It did too look like Daddy's. Daphne lowered her head, pressed it against the brick, and shut her eyes. She half wished she could shut her ears too.

The woman answered, "I guess, you feel slightly— murderous."

But she sounded happy, like she was only teasing.

"You shouldn't be so cocky."

It *was* him.

3

"Us neurotic malcontents, you know, are rarely all that predictable."

Yes, Daddy, no one else. And he wasn't revising any play in there, or making secret-agent plans. He was just doing stuff—with a woman. And that's why he was in this smelly building, why he didn't answer the bell. And that meant now . . .

A voice was yelling inside her head. Gloria back in Cedarhurst.

"It's a girl friend, he's got a girl friend. And he'll never come back. Never."

It had been so long ago, months. Daphne stood by the big tree between her house and Gloria's. She was looking back toward Gloria's, because Mrs. Blumenthal had just told her to go away, shouted it, and without even open-ing the door. Strange. Gloria's mother had never done a thing like that.

Then Mr. Blumenthal, hurrying down their front walk, carrying two suitcases, and all dressed up in bright-blue pants and a gold sports jacket. His new Grand Prix parked in front of the house instead of the driveway, and that was funny too.

Daphne heard a commotion inside their house. Gloria and her mother yelling back and forth: "Don't go out there!" "Yes, I will too!" "You stay in here!" "You can't make me!"

And Gloria rushing out, and trying to yank the car keys out of her father's hand. But he grabbed her arm, held her away with one hand, while he finished opening the trunk with the other.

4

Gloria's face was blotchy and red, like she'd been crying a long time, and she kept saying, "You can't go away, I'm not going to let you, you can't."

He didn't answer.

She turned and grabbed one of his suitcases. But it was too heavy, and all she could do was drag it a little.

He wrenched it right back from her and stowed it in the trunk.

Meanwhile she dashed away to the car door, pushed her arm through the handle, almost up to the elbow, trying to lock herself to it.

He just pulled her arm free, lifted her, and set her down on the grass. "I said I'll visit you in two weeks."

The car varoomed, and he was gone.

Gloria's eyes followed the car till she couldn't see it any more. Then she lay down and kicked one heel viciously into the sod.

Daphne went over to her. "Gloria, get up."

Her answer was to kick again.

How could she make Gloria see this wasn't sensible? "'Cause what about your leather skirt? It'll get dirty. It's brand-new."

"He'll never come back."

Gloria didn't seem to hear.

"He'll never come back, he'll never come back."

Daphne felt sorry for her. She wanted to cheer her up. "Say, come on over to my house."

Gloria's voice was getting tinier. "He'll never never never come back."

It seemed silly to Daphne. Because where would he go? Except Gloria was so upset.

5

Daphne crouched next to her friend. "Why won't he?"

"'Cause it's a girl friend."

"So?"

"So he's got to go to California and sell sportswear. 'Cause you need money for girl friends." Gloria rolled over onto her stomach and got up. "I wish I could kill her. And him too."

But Gloria couldn't ever kill anybody. And Mr. Blumenthal never did come back. Anyway, he hadn't when Daphne moved away from Cedarhurst. So probably he never would. And Gloria was right.

Daphne jumped up. She wanted to get away from this fire escape fast. Clanging, she ran up the metal-slatted stairs. If only these would keep going up and up right into the sky. She didn't care now who heard or saw—if behind one of those windows an enemy agent was aiming at her, or the extortionist she'd seen once on *Private Eye* in a building like this.

Nor did she slow down, even though someone had started calling.

She swung her body over the hot tiled rim and down onto the roof. Panting, she crouched in a shaded corner, then sat.

Gloria never did what she said she would, and her father went to California. So did that mean if Daphne wanted Daddy to stay, she might really have to kill somebody?

CHAPTER 2

Rachel draped her moist towel over the footboard, stretched out on the sagging bed, tucked both pillows under her head, and felt good—very good. It would have been nice if Henry were still here next to her, but having him just a few feet away, muttering while he intensely penciled changes on his script, was warming too. She looked around at the jagged cracks in the walls, the Salvation Army furniture, the grimy window, the dear man, who somewhere else had children and a wife, and thought, how odd—that here in this stuffy slum, with this childlike man, she should feel so content.

She started. She heard a loud pong, pong, pong. So close, on top of her almost. It had to be just outside the window—someone running up or down the fire escape. A junkie? A sneak thief?

She jerked the sheet over her and thought, Henry, do something! Or at least, just react! But she could see he was moving his lips, probably filling his head with imaginary sounds, which doubtless were drowning out the real ones.

"Henry!" she snapped.

A little dazed, he looked up.

Her hand shaking just a bit, she pointed toward the window.

He seemed to absorb her tension and the noise simultaneously, and in a second was raising the shade and poking his head out.

She could see he was twisting his neck upward. "Who is it? What's out there?"

Instead of answering her, though, she heard him yell, "Hey! Hey, you!" Then abruptly he ducked back in, snatched his pants off the radiator, and began thrusting his legs into them.

Why? The clanging footsteps had faded and were gone. Why should he be scrambling into his clothes? Whoever had been out there could be dangerous. He didn't really intend to chase after them, did he?

"God, Henry, who's out there? What are you doing?"

"I don't know. Some kid. I'll be right back," and he tore out of the room. He hadn't even put on his shoes.

She had to stop him, ask him more. She sprang from the bed, but just then heard the door slam. The only thing covering her was a sheet. Hell.

God, could his wife have hired a detective to spy on him? What a grisly thought. Rachel had heard enough about Joanne Beckman to know she couldn't cut it as a wife or a mother. But none of what Henry had groaned and sighed about her had ever indicated she'd stoop to something this sordid. And why should she? Emotionally unstrung, overweight, but she wasn't supposed to be stupid. What would be the *point* of catching her husband *flagrante delicto?* The woman had to know he didn't have the money for much of a divorce settlement.

Rachel began slipping into her underthings, pulling on her stockings. Henry's running off like this was absurd.

8

But then, except for their last half hour together, the whole afternoon had been absurd.

Sonny-James' hillbilly twang booming in via her intercom still reverberated in her mind.

"Miss apple strudel, did ya ever try these here Finlandia coffee beans?" And Laura vainly trying to get rid of him. "Sir, Mrs. Nyland cannot see you today." Laura was as tough a kid as Rachel had ever had in that outer office, but getting rid of a Sonny-James Parker was something else.

Rachel had found him stretched out on the chrome-legged anteroom couch, in the same boots, same great bush of a beard, ringleted curly red hair, perfectly at home, making as if he were oblivious to the fact he'd been gone for three years.

Well, to her he had become a memory, and that's what she meant for him to remain.

"D'you know there is poetry in this here Gomorrah? In its very heart? You seen the sculpture garden at Chase Manhattan Plaza? Meditated there?"

Rachel couldn't help but smile. Half the teen-age girls in America would have fallen at his feet, and a fair number already had. Yet here he was in a mid-Manhattan office, the folk-singing idol, offering her handfuls of Finlandia coffee beans, and refusing to recognize that his advances, his presence even, were grotesque.

"Golly Moses, Ray, you do look goody-good-good. Bulgin' perfect as ever, even if you are thirty-five years old. Cute hat too. Even if it is jes like the rest a them head-up-their-ass New York lady agents."

There'd been no escaping him but to flee the building.

Zipping up her dress, she had an awful thought. Her fingers froze. Could that have been *him* out there? Could he have followed her here?

Once outside the door, Henry's fierce urge to catch that little girl, at least find out definitely who she was, diminished. He lingered in the hall, noticed it smelled of cauliflower, or maybe some Puerto Rican vegetable, fetid. But it was quiet. No scampering-down noises. The child probably had to be still up there.

He shook his head. It still felt thick, packed with nothing that made sense. Could those clambering little legs really have been Daf's? But God, the awful danger, swinging up over the edge of that high roof, five flights up. Just the thought, and his legs felt rubbery. Besides, how could she have gotten here, or found this place? True, Joanne could have sent her. No, but not out on that fire escape.

Shrugging, he rested a hand on the blackish railing, and started up the stairs.

What a kooky day! Rachel, how female, contradictory, capricious, her arriving here after they'd both agreed she wouldn't. And she'd been the one to insist: "Darling, that fleabag's got to be yours, alone, your preserve, a niche for whatever it is that drives you to write things. And not for worrying about your law-firm stuff, or Joanne, or your kids' psyches, or for playing house with me."

"Why can't it be good for both?"

"We'll play. But not there."

Her discipline, self-restraint, so that he could finish his revisions in time, despite the hungry and almost constant tug they both felt toward one another, had thrilled him.

And now, less than a week later, she hadn't been able to stay away.

He chuckled. Hell, enjoy feeling irresistible. You're forty-one. It'll probably never happen again.

At the fifth-floor landing, he looked up the dark flight toward the roof, and his smile dried up. What if Joanne were up there *with* Daf? Hot flickerings of anger darted around in his chest.

CHAPTER 3

Daphne didn't want to think about what had just happened. She didn't want to think about anything. She just wanted to go away from this hot filthy roof.

She couldn't move, though. It was as if her legs wouldn't do what her head told them to. Or maybe her head was all tired too.

If only—if only Miss Kornzweig hadn't made her stay after class.

She saw her chubby, pimply teacher sitting down at the child's desk cater-cornered to hers.

"Now, all we're going to do is talk for a while. I'm not going to punish you."

"You can punish me."

Why had Daf blurted that out? But, then, was the teacher scared too? She'd kind of blinked and swallowed.

"Tell me. Why did you do it?"

"Do what?" Daphne didn't know why she'd stolen that grade book, and changed all the kids' marks to hundreds. Was it so they'd like her better?

The teacher wasn't saying anything. Maybe she just didn't care any more.

"Can I go now? My brother plays baseball. He can't wait long."

The teacher got up. Daf saw the back of her skirt and blouse had to unstick from the seat.

"Daphne, what if I were to promote you to class secretary? I could use your help. Keeping attendance records, and with grades too. Would you like that?"

"I don't fall for psychology."

Miss Kornzweig froze.

Daphne was being nasty now, she knew, but she couldn't seem to stop.

Then the teacher spoke again. "What do you think we should do?"

"Gloria's parents are divorced, but she's still in Cedarhurst."

Daf could see Miss Kornzweig didn't understand. And how could you ever ever explain to her about Cedarhurst?

"Look, I know I'm a stupid pest. Now can I go? I get scared around here. Don't make me walk home alone. Please?"

The teacher pulled up a chair cozily close.

"Don't do that!" And Daf twisted her head away.

Miss Kornzweig looked hurt. "Why?"

"Well, uh, did you ever think of using Arrid, or one of those?"

Racing down the caged-in stairwell, Daphne couldn't believe it was really over, that in another minute the teacher wouldn't catch her.

But then at the bottom, the door to the schoolyard was

locked. She pushed hard, and it still wouldn't open. Just outside she could hear kids playing. Locks, that's all New York is, a monster place for keeping you out, and keeping you in.

Suddenly the unyielding door and the metal grille encasing the stairs swam around in her eyes and became a tremendous cage. Cheeping monkeys were swinging from little bars, popping peanuts into their mouths. And she was in there too, with no way to get out. A class of kids were coming to look at the animals. Then they all saw her. One laughed, then all of them, and they began to stick out their tongues at her.

She charged back up to the main hall, and was skittering past Washington, Lincoln, Martin Luther King, lots of bulletin boards. Up ahead she could begin to see the gleam of daylight pouring in through the front entrance. And as she got closer, it grew brighter, dazzling.

From behind, a voice thundered, "Hey, kid! Where you goin'? Come over heah!"

She wanted desperately to keep running, but the voice was too terrifying.

She stopped and slowly turned. He was so big and black. She couldn't face him, and had to look down at his blue-and-white-striped overalls, his thick-soled high shoes. She couldn't move.

He came closer. She stole a look. He seemed to fill the hall, his head almost up to the ceiling, and getting bigger and bigger.

"You got a note?"

She gasped. She had to shut her eyes.

"You don't, hunh. Then, whut you doin' in heah? . . . Why you runnin'?"

"I—I had to talk with my teacher."

"Gimme that schoolbag!"

Why? What was he talking about?

But before she could think of an answer, he'd grabbed it from her, unbuckled the straps, and was rifling through her books, pencils, jacks, rock specimens, lipstick tubes.

He looked up, not angry any more, and thrust the bag back at her. "Sorry, chile, but dey been robbin' everythin' heah." He made wide, floppy airplane wings with his arms. "Chalk, rubber bands—toilet seats!"

"Can I go now?"

"Next time you's after school"—now he was barking again, like he wanted to wipe out having been nice for a minute—"you 'sposed to have a note, you understan'!"

Vick! He was still waiting. She felt like kissing him to death. She'd spotted his yellow T-shirt and blue baseball cap halfway up the wire-mesh fence, right next to a sign: WARNING, LOITERERS IN VICINITY OF SCHOOL OR TRESPASSERS ON SCHOOL PROPERTY ARE SUBJECT TO ARREST FOR DISORDERLY CONDUCT. He'd climbed up, so he could keep an eye on all the doors at once, but he didn't know the ones opening into the yard were locked now.

She had to run right under him almost, before he heard her and scampered down. She took his arm and pressed it against her cheek. He'd never have let her kiss him, and she had to do something, she was so glad he was still here. After a second, though, he pulled free. So nobody could see, and think he was some kind of sissy.

16

Walking home, she saw an awful sign in a window: TODAY'S SPECIAL, PIGS' TAILS, 25¢ LB. The store was called La Estrella Carniceria Latina. She peered through the glass at the tray of tiny curled-up white things, and said, "Gee, I wonder what those taste like."

"Come on, will you! I gotta tryout for a team. And those guys are going to be older and bigger. And tough."

He stood a few feet ahead, in front of another store. Taped to its window was a huge poster of a Black girl's puffy face. She looked sleepy, or maybe high on drugs. At the bottom it read, "What did you drop into when you dropped out of school?"

They turned a corner, and Spanish music blared from a radio in a brownstone window. The sidewalk was thronged with mustachioed men, darkish women with hair dyed blond and red. They were talking, screeching, flashing gold-specked teeth at each other—sitting on stoops, leaning out windows, lolling against parked cars.

Suddenly a dog with diseased-looking pink patches on its sides was sniffing at Daf's ankle, nuzzling her calf.

"Vickie!" she cried-mewed-moaned.

But he was somewhere ahead, weaving his way through the crowd, and didn't hear.

Then the animal's wet wheezing nose was poking under her dress, licking her thigh, snuffling up between her legs.

Scat! Get away! But the words gagged in her throat and wouldn't come out. Finally she managed to scream, "Annhhhh! Get it away!"

Panting still, the dog backed off by itself. With its

mouth hanging wide open and its nose pointed up, it looked surprised, as if to say, Why the fuss?

But then Vick was there, taking her arm, and pulling her along with him, fast.

Facing them, seated astride the hood of a mottled, rust-riddled car, was a fleshy man in an undershirt. A pock-marked chrome zephyr stuck up between his legs. He was laughing. "Ee teeckle you. Ha ha ha. You no like ee teeckle you?" And a cacophony of squeals and cackles echoed from nearby bumper and fender loungers.

If only she had an atomic aerosol, like Private Eye's, just once she'd squirt it at them, just once.

She remembered stopping just in the middle of crossing Amsterdam.

"Vick, you know Sunday it's Daddy's birthday."

"So?" And he tugged her back into motion.

"He doesn't like New York either. How can you grow strawberries around here?"

Vick could be smart sometimes, but she could see now he didn't catch on at all.

"I'll bet you if we get him a great enough present, he'd say we could move again, away from here."

Vick shook his head and made a face, but didn't talk.

"Don't you make like it's a nutty idea. Because it's not!"

He eyed her. "Daddy's *not* going to pack ten million boxes again, after one month. Besides, he sold the garden tools."

He turned away to look at the dusty pelvises. These were laced into orthotic supports in the Mt. Sinai Surgical Supply window, "Headquarters for Medicare and Medicaid patients."

Daphne waited till they were past the creepy store, and there was nothing much else for him to look away at.

"You got any money?"

"Yeah, some."

"Well, you'll have to give it to me."

"You crazy? I'm saving up for new cleats."

How could she make him see this was a billion times more important than new cleats? What was he looking at now? She followed his gaze to the yellow-and-black fallout-shelter emblem over a doorway, then slipped her hand into his.

"You need those cleats real real bad?"

He smiled. He could never, she knew, stay mad at her for too very long.

"What," he asked, "do you want to get him?"

"I don't know. Except it's got to be fantastic."

"I only got thirteen and a half dollars."

"But would you give it?"

He pushed open the door to their building, massive decorative iron grille over glass. They ambled on through the gloomy tiled vestibule.

This time he hadn't told her she was crazy and to bug off, which meant that maybe—maybe he'd understood, sometimes she could be right, even if she was younger and smaller.

It felt so uncomfortable trying to get the words out to ask again, but she *had* to.

"So, *would* you?"

They'd reached the elevator. He pressed the button, and still didn't answer.

If she sounded all ready to start crying, maybe she could dare again.

"Even if it's only for a chance of moving back, even then, wouldn't that be worth it? . . . Please?"

It seemed like an hour, and then he shrugged. "Aw, most guys here in the city, they don't even wear cleats anyway."

Yes, that was yes!

She locked her arms around Vick from the rear, which was the only way she could, with him facing the elevator so closely. Just then the porthole of light appeared, and the door creaked open.

Daf stood in the front hall outside her mother's door, wanting to go in, but afraid. Mom was typing. Daf could hear the slow tat-tat-tapping. It was nice Mom was home this early. Still, when it was term papers, Mom could get screaming mad so easy. You never knew how she might be.

Vick, clutching his baseball mitt and a fistful of cookies, and with a new milk smudge around his lips, charged past, then stopped.

"Watcha standing there for?"

"Sh-h-h-h!"

Daf glided past the barrels and cartons, which had yet to be unpacked, right up to her brother, and pleaded, "She's typing."

"So?"

Shaking his head at her screwy fearfulness, he undid both locks, said, "Geez," and went out.

Daphne listened. She was hoping the tat-tat-tats would stop for a minute. Finally they did. She raised her knuckles, lowered them, took a breath, raised them again, and knocked.

"What is it, dear?"

Mom didn't sound angry. Daphne eased open the door. The air conditioner was throbbing, and she felt coolness, which was great, except for the stale refrigerated smoke smell.

Her mother said, "Hi," and smiled.

Daf's fears zipped away. A gladness swelled inside her.

Mom was in her mini-toga pajamas, which made her look sagging and more overweight even than she was. A cigarette drooped from her lips. Clustered all around her were the same old wobbly piles of books, packages of typing paper, yellow paper, carbon paper. And those white cards were lined up in long silly rows on her desk, both beds, and on the floor too.

Daf came closer, brushing past the yet-to-be-unpacked cartons, which here too were stacked against the wall.

"Mom, can I ask you something?"

"Sure. First bring me a glass of water, though, would you? This new diet calls for eight big glasses a day. And remember the door, the air conditioner."

In the kitchen Daphne climbed up on a stool to get down one of the big glasses. She took out the ice-cube tray too.

Mom could be such a pain, always making you do this

and do that. Now, though, you had to keep her happy. It was too important.

"Ice too? My, my. Thank you. Now, sweetie, please, be quick. Racine and Seneca here are due tomorrow, and God knows, I need every minute."

"Well, Sunday . . ." Daf didn't know why saying this was hard, but it was. She gripped the bedpost, hung from it kind of with one hand. ". . . Daddy's birthday. What can I get him?"

Then she swayed a little, waiting for an answer.

Suddenly her mother snapped, "Careful!"

Daf saw she'd jostled the bed. A few index cards might have moved. She let go and stood up straight.

"So can you think of something, something he'd be wild about?"

She saw her mother's eyes slip back to the typewriter.

"Yes, we'll have to think about that. Tell me, did you have a good day in school, dear?"

"That's not what I asked you about."

Geez, why'd she raise her voice? That wasn't smart.

"Something must have happened, Daf. Tell me."

"You never hear what I say!" Hell, now she *was* shouting. Tears were starting to come, and she didn't want to cry, not here.

Bursting into her own room, Daphne threw herself on her canopy bed, snatched Oscar, her penguin who had an orange beak and feet, and held him tight.

She heard her mother at the door. This place wouldn't really feel like her room until Daddy unpacked the canopy and put it back up overhead. Then Mom was crouching alongside, but Daf didn't want to look at her.

Something was touching, Mom trying to stroke her hair.

Daphne rolled away. Who wanted to love her, if she always said you were wrong? But Mom moved too, still staying close.

Maybe—maybe she did want to hear. "Mom, how much would it cost to buy a theater?"

"A little marionette theater?"

"No, like Radio City."

Mom was wrinkling her forehead.

Why? What was so hard about this? "My government bond, the one Grandma Edna said would get to be more money every year . . . well, did it?"

Her mother smiled and got up, like everything was all settled and happy now. "Daffy, can we save this until tomorrow?"

Daphne wanted to scream, "Why can't you ever do one thing I ask you?" But all that came out of her mouth was, "I guess so."

She pressed her face down into the pillow.

Her mother started out. Then Daf heard her stop.

"You know, we could use some bread for supper. Would you run down to . . ."

Daphne jerked her head up and interrupted, "No, I want it."

"What, dear? Bread?"

"The bond. Daddy's birthday."

"You want to give him your bond?"

"A theater. Radio City."

"Daf, we'll talk about it tomorrow."

Even though her brows were knitted up, Mom's voice

sounded like maybe she meant it. "Will you swear to get it for me?"

Daf saw her mother's hand clench around the doorknob tightly.

"Dear, Radio City would cost more than you . . ."

"But Vick's chipping in too."

"Sweetie, your grandmother never intended . . ."

"*If it's mine, why can't I have it?*"

Mom shut her eyes, wiped her forehead with the mini-toga hem, then kind of looked everywhere but at Daphne. She seemed to stop on Daddy's photo, the one of him sitting cross-legged on the grass, on top of Daf's dresser. There weren't any pictures hung up on the wall yet, so it had to be that one.

Mom wet her lips, like hesitating. "How—how would you like to go ask your father what *he'd* like for his birthday?"

"Now?" Would Mom really let her? "All the way downtown?"

"He's just a few blocks from here. Yes, he's rented a room. He's doing some last-minute revisions there on this play of his."

"Really?" That sounded so weird.

Her mother nodded.

"But he never told me. Is it—secret?"

But, then, maybe *that's* where it was, hidden in that room, the real secret of why they'd moved to New York.

Music, the scary drumbeats and jumpy high notes of the *International Secret Mission* theme began to ring in her head. Then her father, only in TV black and white—she could half see him. He was swinging the big head-

24

quarters clock away from the wall, and pressing the special button. Bookshelf walls revolved away. Black shades sealing the windows descended. The floor-to-ceiling map lit up. Suddenly there was the crew too: the bravest, swingingest gang of counter-agents in America, going to listen to her daddy.

He was pinpointing the mission objective with a long poker. "Now our enemy's top-secret germ-warfare laboratory is located here. You'll find, however, that it is surrounded and protected by . . ."

"He'll be pleased . . ." Her mother drowned her father out and vanished everything away . . . "you're so fired up about his birthday."

This, Daphne decided, if it was true, could be such a fantastic secret that even Mom wouldn't know about it.

But—but what if Daddy might not want her to know about it either? "So if I just come there, all of a sudden, he won't be mad?"

"Why should he be?"

Sure. Daf would swear not to tell: no one, nowhere, no matter what they did to her. Even torture, or brainwashing.

Back in Mom and Dad's bedroom, she struggled with the lid of a big can. Finally she inched it off, and stuffed a few handfuls of the stuff into a clear plastic baggie.

"Now," Mom asked, "what are you doing?"

Daf smiled. "Taking him a little tobacco."

Joanne thumbed through card after card, searching for the footnote backup on Hippolytus' gory death. It began,

25

she thought, with a first line about the sea vomiting up a raging monster. Could it have gotten mixed with the stack on the bed? Turning there from the desk, her eyes stopped on the window.

She felt a sudden urge to jump up, push open the window, yell down to Daphne, stop her. Henry wouldn't take time for the child. He'd be annoyed, resentful. Daf would be crushed. But—if now she dragged Daf back, the kid would be furious, altogether impossible. Joanne's head throbbed just above her eyes. Why—*why* did this basically sweet girl *have* to be such a problem? No, not fair. Not her fault, really . . . Henry, damn him!

Joanne could still see him sitting with the *Times* in his hands. It'd been only last night. Quivering, choked up, speaking words that had ripped into her like bullets. "Insensitive, unfeeling, stupefied, self-immolated, mountainous slob!" So vicious. Unlike him. And just because she'd asked that he hang a few pictures . . . Well, actually it had been more like, "How can you just sit there, not lifting a finger, week after week, and let us live in a—warehouse, a pigsty? Can't you at least . . . ?" True, she was not interested in his play of plays, and all his little agonies about it. But did he give two hoots about her work, or the never-ending tension of these children, in this city?

Out of the blue she remembered great, wonderful swells of pride, when Henry would plead so brilliantly for some insane protester. Eight years ago? Ten? A thousand? Had she *really* felt them?

After this paper, maybe next week, she and Henry would have to thrash out some agreement, or disagreement. Daf'll be all right. The kid's made of steel.

Daphne looked up, above the doorway to the high windows, and onto the roof. The building looked like all the others on this block: old, dirtyish, ordinary, a perfect place probably for secret agents. Again she checked the number over the door and compared it with the one on her crumpled piece of paper. Lightninglike, she swung about and looked backward. No surveillance. No one ducked into a doorway or behind a car.

Walking up the dimly lit stairs, she heard a woman yelling, "Get out, get out, you get the hell out!" And then a door slammed. Footsteps above began pounding downward. Daphne flattened herself against the wall. The footsteps were loud, almost on top of her. She held her breath. A skinny teen-age boy hurtled past, as if she weren't even there.

At the third-floor landing, Daphne stopped, opened the baggie and sniffed the tobacco. It was such a good smell. It made her feel Daddy *had* to be close by.

She peered up at a door marking. Chips of the number and letter were missing, but still it was readable. No, 4C wasn't right. She tiptoed to the opposite door: 4D. If only there hadn't been any 4D, then this would have been the wrong building, and she could have left.

Ever so gently she touched her forefinger to the bell. It would never ring, though, unless she plunged forward. She bit her lip, shut her eyes, and pushed.

The instant she heard the buzz, her finger flew back. She edged to the stairway, poised to race back down.

What if that door was wired to explode in case someone rang at the wrong time? But it hadn't. And Daddy, after all, could be in the bathroom, or busy wearing earphones.

She slipped back to the door, placed her finger in position, and again propelled it forward.

No one was answering, and she couldn't hold her breath any more.

At the window there was more light. She glided over and rechecked her slip of paper. 4D was right. Then, why had Mom insisted, "Yes, he'll definitely be there."?

The window surrounded by dark wall was so very like a TV screen. She shut her eyes, and heard the *Private Eye* theme. Just a few nights ago, she remembered seeing him out in a hallway exactly like this one. And then inside, behind the door—now Daphne could see it so clearly—the scarface extortionist, wearing a black jumpsuit, smiling cruelly, and slapping the frizzy blonde, who kept pleading with him not to, and crying.

The same woman, one of her eyes swollen and black, was still sobbing, after the commercial. Only now Private Eye was sitting across from her. You could see talking was causing her pain, but still she kept trying. "The bum. You'll never get in there. He's got the door wired with bombs." Private Eye didn't say anything. All he did was nod, but like he knew exactly what to do. Next, Daf saw him catfooting it down the fire escape.

Daphne shook her head just once, but hard. The grimy window stopped being a TV screen and became a window again. Looking back toward 4D, she saw it was still closed and quiet. She turned toward the ascending stairs, and began scampering upward.

Over the rim of the roof, looking down, she felt sort of punched in the stomach. Fire escapes were supposed to go gradual, like real stairs, not a steep awful straight-down ladder. Private Eye even didn't have to go down one like this.

She stepped back. The sun was broiling, but her hands felt so cold.

Then she took a second look. The monkey ladder was only to the first landing. After that, the fourth was only one more flight, and that one would be regular diagonal stairs, with a railing. Still, looking down was hard. Splotches of red, geraniums somewhere, and millions of black slats dizzyingly swam up at her.

She shut her eyes. She remembered the secretary once, waiting for Private Eye, out on a ledge, just as high, narrow, loads more dangerous. So who said you had to be a man?

She took off her shoes. Daddy might even be hurt, or a prisoner, and need help. The tobacco she tucked down her undervest, then gripped the sooty rails, and started to climb up, and fast over the edge, so it would be too late to chicken out.

Lowering herself slowly, carefully, the skinny steel rungs pressed painfully into her soles, and the side rails into her hands.

She stopped. What if the scarface was inside a window, maybe just opposite, and aiming a pistol at her? It'd have a silencer. No one would hear. She'd fall. No one would even know what had happened.

She tried to hurry. The radio began to get loud. "It's going deep, deep into left field." It drowned out her killer daydream. "It's a home run! Beautiful, wicked slash, old

Whitey's fifth of the season!" She crumbled onto the fifth-story slatted platform, gasping.

An airplane droned by overhead.

Yes, a radio—she wished there were a good loud one here on this roof now too. Looking at the toothpicky TV antennas which stuck up everywhere at odd angles, Daphne remembered more things.

Daddy, she'd imagined, was going to be so surprised and glad she'd come, he wasn't going to care about her being all dirty, or out on the fire escape. And right away, he'd do everything, move right back to Cedarhurst and no more New York.

But now—now she'd need a million radios, not just one, to drown all that out.

CHAPTER 4

Still crouched in her corner, Daf heard the stairwell door squeak open. Private Eye, she knew, wouldn't just stick here like a dead duck. He'd make a running leap over to the next house's roof. Now, though, what good would that do—if Daddy was going away like Mr. Blumenthal, forever?

She saw her father shade his eyes and scan the sooty expanse. Maybe, because she was all in the shade, he wouldn't ever see her.

"Little girl?" he called. "Anyone up here? Daf?"

No, he wasn't leaving. She saw him begin moving across the roof, picking his way through the clotheslines and antennas. Then he was hopping and jumping, so strangely.

Of course! His feet were bare, so he probably was trying to stay off the globs of melted tar.

Suddenly he was sprinting toward her band of shade. He'd seen her, he must have.

She lowered her head. She didn't want to look at him.

"Daf, is that you?"

His voice was close. Then it came right next to her. "Daf?"

She had to look up at him. And she hadn't been able to stop her stupid tears either.

Was he dizzy? Or sick? She saw him leaning against the waist-high wall, half propping himself up with his hand, and breathing in a lot of air.

Then he knelt and reached to draw her to him.

She stiffened. She didn't want to touch him.

He didn't care, though. She felt herself being lifted and held. Still, she kept her hands glued to her sides.

"Hey, it's me," he said. "Yeah, me."

His chest suddenly became the perfect place. She wished she could burrow in, and hide inside there.

Henry's eyes retraversed the steaming stretch of roof. No, the child was alone. No Joanne. Still, this had to be somewhat her responsibility. Or—or was it more his?

Ignoring the searing heat underfoot, he walked with Daf slowly to the stairs.

Why did she come here? What prompted her to? What did she actually see? What psychological effect might this ultimately have on her? Why—out on that fire escape? Questions in an unceasing continuum kept clicking into his mind, and then answers, more and more wild and impossible. Now, though, was not, he decided, the time to try and pin it all down.

His handkerchief, thank God, was still in his pants. He stopped and held it to her nose.

Coming down the flight of steps leading to the ground floor, Daphne began studying her father's toes, how they rippled a little as they landed on each tread.

32

"Where," she asked, "are your shoes?"

"I guess I was in a hurry."

He really ought, he thought, to walk her back home, spend the rest of the day with her. Eleven actors, though, were expecting that new scene at seven. And Rachel, up there alone, and probably worried sick.

"Daf," he *had* to ask, "why did you come here?"

"I wanted to ask you something. But it was silly."

She shot her hand forward and pulled open the front door. In another minute, maybe, she could get away from here, and then he wouldn't be able to make her talk about that horrible stuff.

Out on the stoop, though, she remembered something important. "You won't tell Mommy I climbed out on the fire escape, will you?"

"No."

He was stunned. Of all things, now—fear of her mother?

"See, I had to know if it was the right apartment. 'Cause no one answered."

"Did Mommy send you with a message for me?"

"No."

"She just gave you this address, because you wanted to ask me something?"

"Un-hunh. Can I go now?"

"What—what are you going to tell her you found?"

"I guess, that no one answered."

He slowly shook his head, amazed at her innate discretion. She could, he now felt sure, make it home alone too.

"Daf, we'll have a big talk about everything, suppertime."

"Mommy said you weren't coming tonight."

"I said we'll talk. Maybe it will be a little later on in the evening, though."

"Bye."

Down the last steps she hurried.

He wanted to follow, catch her arm, hug her. Something, though, held him back.

Henry slogged back up. He felt drained, depressed. Should he tell Rachel, or make up some story? God knows, her first formal meeting with the child, when it came—and that wouldn't be too far off—would be awkward enough, without this to thrash over.

Yet if Daf knew just the two of them shared this secret, and Rachel wasn't in on it, wouldn't that, in a way, be betraying Rachel?

On the other hand, though, how could this help but prejudice Rachel against Daf? And before too very long she'd be the child's stepmother.

His head hurt. Maybe . . . was this the time to propose?

Daphne smelled spices and baking dough. Her mouth watered. The aroma grew stronger as she got closer to the corner. She saw two small boys perched on stools at a counter, above them a PIZZA sign. The man served them, and they picked up wedges bigger than their faces and chomped into them. Their chins and noses got all smeared with runny cheese and tomato. She wished she had a quarter. One of the boys noticed her staring at them. She felt embarrassed and walked on.

34

She dawdled before a building whose walls were coated with posters. It was an old walk-up, probably about to be wrecked. She could tell, because its front door and windows were sealed with sheet metal. The ads were for boxing matches, the circus, a veterans' approved beauty-culture school, and something called Z. Further along, she saw a big blue-and-yellow poster, heralding a RHYTHM AND BLUES SWINGARAMA, THREE GREAT ORCHESTRAS. Running down its side was a picture of a woman singer in a low-cut gown.

Hadn't Daf seen this Maria Concepcion on TV? On Dean Martin maybe? She went right up close, to really see her face. It was in blue ink, full of wavy little lines, awfully blurry. Suddenly it seemed familiar. Was it the same face she'd seen on the fire escape? Then the singer's gown was gone. She was naked too.

Daphne turned away. She didn't want to look at the stupid poster, which was nothing but a dumb daydream anyway. And then the proof that it had to be a daydream was seeing Gloria. There she was, half real and half see-through, lying on the sidewalk and kicking, just the way she had in Cedarhurst that time, yelling, "She's a girl friend, a girl friend. Your father has a girl friend!"

"She is not!" Daphne yelled right back. "Well, I don't have proof, do I?"

A patrol car cruised past. Gloria disappeared.

Daf tried to think, What would Private Eye do now? She sucked her thumbnail, glanced back toward the poster.

Hey, yeah, she's the suspect. And with suspects, you always have to . . . follow them, find out, like, where they live . . .

Daphne rushed back toward the pizza stand. Just after turning the corner, she had to move off the sidewalk to get around a potsy game.

The building's entrance became only three houses away, and she stopped. She needed a lookout. The neighboring stoops didn't look too hot. She spied a slatted U-haul attached to a parked car, and darted behind it.

Crouching, she watched that door. Soon her legs ached. She changed to a kneeling position, then to a crouch again. A spiffy Black man kept rambling up and down the sidewalk, every so often slapping people's hands, and getting slapped in return by them.

Was he a pusher? But then he even did the same thing with a policeman. What did that mean?

It was her! Daf knew right away. Her clothes all matched so cool, and like in a magazine.

The woman, reaching the sidewalk, stopped and looked both ways, then moved out into the street.

Daphne edged around to the back of the U-haul to stay out of sight. The woman, she saw, was sticking her hand up into the air, trying to hail a taxi.

Private Eye was always diving into cabs. "Follow that car. Stay with him, and you make a hundred bucks." Then you'd hear the engine varoom and the tires squeal.

But what if you didn't have any hundred bucks? Daphne scooped out her pocket. Her hand held a chipped Chiclet, a bobby pin and two pennies. Oh yes, and there was the tobacco in her undervest. She pushed the Chiclet into her mouth. Maybe she could trade the tobacco for a taxicab ride. "Follow that car, and you get . . ."

But then the woman was back on the sidewalk, and walking. No more cabs were coming.

Daphne waited until the woman reached the lamp-post halfway to the corner. Following her, she slipped from parked car to parked car.

At the pizza corner, the lady stopped and just stood. Other people, Daphne saw, were standing too. Then she saw the yellow curb and the bus sign. Hell, she didn't have the money for that either.

Unless—unless maybe a bus wouldn't be so impossible. Lots of kids sneaked buses. Once with Vick she'd had a token all ready, and someone had pushed her past the money box, and the driver never said boo.

Rapidly she surveyed the cluster of waiting people. The best possibility, she decided, was a darkish, probably Puerto Rican, lady, fat as a house, who also had two crammed shopping bags.

Two blocks up, she saw the bus. It looked tiny, green and cute. Then it came closer, grew bigger and bigger, into a monster almost, that would have to crush down on them. Everyone else, though, was just fishing out their change.

People pressed around the door. Daphne, standing apart, counted to three, took a breath, and pushed forward, until she was touching the Spanish woman's skirt, insinuating herself almost under her arm, stepping aboard right with her, smelling her strong sour smell.

Inside now, Daf hunched, trying to make herself tiny as the shopping bag. Her heart sounded like it was booming louder than the coin machine or the engine. She had to shut her eyes.

Then she felt the bus lurch and begin to move. The driver couldn't have seen her—unless . . . Was he heading straight to the police station, but not telling anyone?

37

She slithered past the fat Latin lady, and sneaked a look back. The driver was covered up behind a lot of people. The bus suddenly jolted to a halt. Why? She was terrified. Was he going to ask a policeman to pull her off?

She leaned way across someone's seat, and saw a double-parked truck. Everyone was honking, the bus too. Daphne exhaled. Maybe soon her heart would get quiet.

The fire-escape lady, Daf saw, was sitting. She looked graceful, not like the other sweaty people all around. Her legs tapered so nicely, and her ankles too. Not like Mom's diet with her "eight big glasses of water a day."

Should she, Daf wondered, just tail her secretly, or try and begin investigating right now? Private Eye probably'd take the next seat, start talking about the humidity, and in two minutes he'd get half the clues.

There *was* an empty seat next to the lady. Daf bit her lip, hesitating.

Suddenly the lady rose and crossed over to the rear door.

Daphne rushed off too, but through the front door. Straight across the sidewalk she sauntered into the doorway of a closed real-estate/insurance store, and pretended to look at two dead plants in the window. She felt thirsty. And it would be getting dark soon. Which is when it could get hard to follow people, and when muggers were supposed to come out.

As nonchalantly as she could, she turned. The lady, she saw, was almost across the avenue.

At the other side, the lady stopped, turned, and looked up the street. Daphne swung in the same direction.

A bus, a crosstown, was coming, and just a block away! Could you ever sneak in two times? . . . No, now she'd have to quit.

Daphne flew across the street, halting one square of pavement away from the lady. No one else, only she, was waiting.

It'd be impossible, unless . . .

Daf turned and saw the bus was almost upon them.

No, this would be *the* only way.

Her eyes fixed down on the lady's blue suede shoes, Daf took a giant step right next to her and blurted, "Could you lend me thirty-five cents or a token? I'll pay you back, honest. I'll bring it to your house tomorrow, early, before I even leave for school." Daf forced herself to look up. "Okay?"

The lady smiled. "I think that can be arranged."

Daf smiled too.

While the woman was paying, it got scary again. They were moving to a seat, and Daf tried hard to think of the answer. There was one question this lady had almost got to ask.

"What happened to *your* carfare?"

"See, I didn't spend it on ice cream or anything like that. See, I was jumped by some Spanish kids. They cleaned me out."

Daf could tell it had worked!—from the way the woman looked down at the dirt all over her dress.

"Were you hurt?"

"A little. Not much."

Daf suddenly thought of something else wrong. Talking now to this woman could be terrible, because after

39

this, how could Daf ever follow her again and not be recognized?

"Would you write me down your address, so I could bring you the thirty-five cents?"

The woman patted her knee. "Oh, forget it."

"But I can't. I'm not allowed to take money. From anybody. My mother's very strict."

"Don't tell her."

"Yeah, but, you know, I'm terrible at telling lies."

The woman smiled again.

Did that mean she felt sorry for you, or that she knew it was a lie?

"Four seventy-nine East Sixty-eighth."

Great! Here it was, the first clue, and already she'd gotten it. Maybe she'd write Private Eye, and now he'd let her be one of his partners too.

God, she couldn't see any more buildings up ahead. They were so close to driving through Central Park. She'd be walking and walking forever, if she didn't get off. And in the dark too.

Abruptly she jumped up and said, "Bye," then hurried to the exit.

The bus stopped.

Suddenly she remembered something, the most important thing. "Oh!" she called back, "what's your name?"

"Mrs. Nyland."

"Don't worry. I'll pay you back."

Stepping down into the street, Daf kept repeating it to herself, "Four seventy-nine East Sixty-eighth, four seventy-nine East Sixty-eighth. Mrs. Nyland, Mrs. Nyland . . .

Now if she ever had to, she'd pay her back all right.

CHAPTER 5

Her legs ached from walking so far.

At a corner, looking up at the traffic light, Daf noticed the street lamp. The cars coming down Central Park West, she realized, were glowing too. A set of headlights glared into her eyes.

Crossing, she looked over toward the park. Just a minute ago, it seemed, everything had been green. Now all was a jumble of black shapes. Night so quick. Walk faster, she decided. She tried to. At every step, though, the pavement felt like it was hammering at her right through her soles.

A bench? They were, she knew, over there along the park wall, but so hard to see. One under a street light stood out, glowed even. But—what if right next to it was some creep with an ice pick?

The curb? Sit there? Her dress was so ucky already, a little more dirt wouldn't matter. It would look awful queer, though.

She edged over to a fire hydrant, half sat and half leaned. Some of the ache left her legs, but now her tummy hurt even more. She had to pee something terrible. Pressing down with her hand helped a little.

Just ahead was a marquee. Fontainebleau Arms. Abreast of the building's thick glass doors, she slowed down. Within, she could see a gurgling fountain, and around it, chairs, velvety-looking settees, and no one sitting on any of them. Then a gray-blue uniform blocked it off. A doorman. Daf knew now it had to be air-conditioned in there too. He was wearing his jacket and a tie. Would he let her in, to rest, just for a little while? She looked at his face. His mouth was clamped shut, mean-looking, like if she came even one step closer, he was ready to yell, "You filthy brat, get out of here. Don't you come *near* this lobby!" Like he even might try and hit her too.

At Amsterdam, only a half a block still to go, she stumbled, but just managed to keep from scraping her knees. She eyed the curb, then sank down, and leaned back against the traffic-light stanchion. In her whole life she'd never had to pee so badly. And pressing her tum wasn't giving relief any more.

People crossing did pause and stare at her, but she didn't care. A police car glided to a halt across the street, double parked. She waited. A loud bull horn commanding her to get up, a spotlight blinding her, handcuffs. It just drove away, though.

"Daf? That you?"

Vickie, his voice? She looked up. Yes, really him. She hugged his legs.

He crouched. "You all right?"

"No, I've got to pee."

"Boy"—he shook his head grimly—"is Mommy going to give it to you."

42

"Vick, if you were going to run away, where would you run to?"

"Hunh, me?"

The Gem movie theater, she thought, would be such a great place. Watching color pictures, eating Crackerjacks, forever. Except, they'd throw you out when the lights came on. Maybe Grandma Edna's. No, she was as bad as Mom, bossing all the time. And besides, she'd tell.

Vick took her arm and was trying to help her up. "Come on, Daf. You can't just stay here, you know."

"I don't want Daddy to go away."

Vick, startled, froze for a second. But then he remembered she'd been pretty screwball this afternoon too. And right now, the thing he had to do was get her home.

"You want to wait here? Daddy's out looking for you too. I'll get him." And he rose.

"No!"

She sprang up and clutched his arm. "Don't get him."

"Okay."

"Please?"

"I only asked if *you* wanted me to."

"I don't."

"Well, come on, then." And he tugged a bit to get her started.

She wouldn't budge.

"Don't you understand? We've got to do something. So Daddy won't go away."

His eyes widened.

"Like Mr. Blumenthal, don't you remember?"

Maybe she'd caught a disease, some kind of germ that gets you in the head.

"'Cause he's got a girl friend. But if you tell anyone, I'll kill you, and I'll never talk to you again."

Could someone have slugged her, and she'd been unconscious, and had a nightmare?

She plunked herself down on the curb again.

He didn't know what to do.

"So do you promise?"

"Promise what?"

"'Cause we might even have to kill that girl friend. So do you?"

"Sure, Daf." It didn't matter, he decided, what he said.

She let him take her hand.

Walking, trying not to limp, she spotted someone hurrying toward them, then breaking into a run.

Daddy! "Don't forget," she whispered fiercely to her brother, "you promised!"

Hairy warm arms encircled her. Even the sharp jab of Daddy's belt buckle sticking into her felt good.

"Come."

"My feet hurt."

His strength quickly was under her knees, her shoulders. He lifted, cradled her against his chest, and he was walking.

"Daddy, aren't I too heavy?"

"You certainly are."

She felt herself slipping, and he jostled her for a better grip.

"Don't let me fall."

"Why shouldn't I?"

"Don't tease me."

He kissed her.

She closed her eyes. If only she could stay this way, next to him, forever.

Daddy stopped, and she heard a creak—Vickie opening the front door probably. Yes, she felt herself rising, Daddy going up the front step. Definitely they were inside, because it was cooler, and the stale smell, and when the door clicked shut behind, the street noises were gone.

Clack, clack, clackety, clackety! The tiled floor and walls suddenly echoed with running footsteps, coming closer, louder. Daf pressed her eyes shut even more tightly. Mom, it almost definitely had to be her.

"Why're you carrying her? What's wrong? Where was she? Daf, you all right?"

"She's tired," her father answered.

Maybe, Daf thought, she could get everyone to believe she was sleeping.

Vick, trying to forestall the explosion he sensed might come, piped in, "She's got to pee."

"Daphne"—Mom's voice was tougher, more demanding —"answer me."

Maybe her father would say something, and she wouldn't have to. She'd nudge him. But first she'd have to sneak a look and find out where Mom was standing.

The Black couple, right here, waiting for the elevator too. How great! She was saved—at least till they got upstairs.

Sure enough, everyone did stop speaking. Boy, the arguments her parents had had back in Cedarhurst. How they'd clammed up then too, the second she or Vick came into the room.

"They're going to take over that whole building," Mom would shriek, "and then what good is your marvelous rent control? You want your kids' playmates *all* to be Black?"

"Joanne, you're wrong."

"They'll be persecuted."

"You're the one who wants to be close to Columbia."

"But not in a building with *them*."

"It happens to be the best we can afford."

"Wait. Just wait till one of us gets slashed. With a razor."

All the way up, no one even coughed.

Soon as Mom opened the apartment, Daf scrambled into the bathroom and locked it. Peeing, she could hear them, huddling right outside the door.

"Go away!"

They shuffled off, but their voices still came through, quietly snapping back and forth.

When she entered the living room, they weren't talking any more. Everyone was sitting separately. It was a strange sight, the furniture arranged in the right places, but with no pictures on the walls, or curtains, or knick-knacks on the piano—it could almost be a high-ranking Kremlin secret-police office.

Mom's hand clamped around her wrist tight.

"I want to know exactly what you've been doing, why you didn't come home."

That meant Daddy hadn't told her anything. So she couldn't either.

Her father took her mother's hand and pulled it away. Daf massaged her wrist.

Mom hardly seemed to notice what he'd done. She just stared at Daf and was breathing more and more heavily.

Daf took the glass of milk her father held out to her, and gulped down a few good swallows.

Mom, Daf could see, was trying to be patient. But every second that passed, Mom was twisting her fingers more, biting down on her lip, and looking steaming, as if any minute she'd surely boil over.

Vick, always trying to cheer things up, said, "You look sort of like a clown, with those big milky-white lips."

"Minstrel," Dad corrected.

"Now"—Mom couldn't hold it in any more—"*where were you?*"

Daf panicked. She could usually think of a good story faster than anyone. Why not now?

"Joanne, maybe she's hungry."

Why, Daf tried to figure, *couldn't* he tell her the truth?

Mom turned from her to Daddy. "Yes, undercut me every time. I'm not permissive." The sarcasm in her voice was razor-edged. "Well, I do not intend to have my kids land up in children's court, with the rest of the animals around here!"

Her father didn't answer. She'd have to think of something fast.

"Why are you so filthy?" Mom's voice was abruptly gentler, pleading almost. "Your dress torn, almost three hours late for supper. Why?"

"Can I have a sandwich?"

"I asked you a question."

"I'm hungry."

"Want me," Vick offered, "to make her a peanut butter and jelly or something?"

"Don't interrupt!"

"Well," Daf slowly began, "you know I went to find Daddy."

"And you couldn't find him?"

Daddy must have told her *something*. But what? She'd have to take a chance.

"Well, no."

"So then what did you do?"

She'd guessed right! But there was no time to enjoy feeling good, 'cause now she'd have to make up the rest.

"I thought maybe I could find him in the park."

Immediately Daf spotted the doubt in her mother's eyes.

"He likes trees."

"And you went there?"

It was hopeless. Now no matter what she said, Daf knew Mom wouldn't believe it. Still, maybe . . . she had to try.

"See, at one of the benches I met this man with only one leg. He was a hunchback. He took out a lot of change and asked if I could get him a Good Humor, 'cause he couldn't walk too good. I should buy one for myself too, he said. Then after I came back, sitting next to him, eating it, he pulled out a long pointy injection needle. And then the next thing was, I just woke up on the sidewalk and came home."

Joanne gasped, and then, Whaaap!

The whole side of Daf's face burned from the slap.

48

"*Now I want the truth!*"

"Leave me alone!"

Her cheek smarting still, Daf waited, terrified. In a second there could come a whole downpour of slaps.

"*Why* do you lie to me?"

Daf was surprised. Her mother's voice had become so different, gentle. Mom, she saw, was now leaning against the door molding, weakly, as if her fury in a flash had all melted away.

Joanne, waiting for an answer, one she sensed/knew she wouldn't get, felt drained, beaten. Could Daf have done all this to her on purpose? No. But still these lost hours were a fact. The term paper now could not make it in for the deadline. She would be knocked down at least one whole grade point.

But that was nothing. Piddling, compared to the realization suddenly flooding her that this child, her own Daphne, wouldn't even talk with her.

"Why"—Joanne was all but begging—"won't you trust me?"

Daf felt badly, sorry she'd lied, sorry for Mom too. It was strange.

"Why?"

"Who says I don't trust you?"

Mom's face got all contorted, as if she were crying and at the same time forcing herself not to. Then she rushed out of the room.

"Vick," Dad softly urged, "go keep your mom company for a while."

He nodded and went.

Daphne looked up at her father. "Did I tell her . . . like you wanted me to?"

Henry felt slimy. He had to reject this woman. She couldn't be a wife for him. But it got him in the craw, helping turn her own child so against her too.

"Daf, you've got to . . . love your mother."

"But *did* I, Daddy?"

Henry sighed. How ravenous she was for a bit of praise. And in a weird way she deserved it.

"Yes, Daf."

She smiled. Now he would never have to leave. See, hadn't she just proved what a reliable pal she could be?

But then she saw him look at his watch.

CHAPTER 6

"More?"

"Oh no, Daddy, I couldn't."

Daphne laid the oversized shrimp, whose sweet and pungent sauce she'd been licking off, back on her plate, and rested her head against the side of the restaurant booth. An hour ago, or whenever they'd first walked into this bustling, aromatic room, with its Japanese-made Chinese lanterns and its plastic bas-relief pagodas on the walls, the only thing she had let herself think about was food. Which had been easy, because she had really been hungry. Visions of spareribs dipped in duck sauce, crispy egg rolls, casseroles of steaming lobster chunks, had all but crowded from her head the real reason they'd come here. As the tiny waiter took away the soup plates, though, she'd noticed how careful he'd had to be with her father's. It was full. Daddy, she'd realized, must have hardly tasted his soup, and just then he'd ordered another martini, his third at least. From then on, even though she'd still done a lot of eating, between mouthfuls and a little talk about school stuff, she'd also been thinking. Should she ask him what was going to happen? About that woman? Did she dare? Or would it be better maybe to wait, and let him go first?

She'd stopped eating, and he had too. But neither of them was saying anything. It was getting to feel uncomfortable.

She had an idea. It would be cute. "How come," she asked, "the Chinese are always starving, when they have such good food?"

And he *did* smile!

She smiled back.

"Feel like some dessert, dear, almond cookies, ice cream, kumquats, jello?"

"Could I taste your martini?"

Cocking his head at an odd angle, he peered down at it, almost as if surprised it was there.

"You've had so many tonight," she persisted. "Please?"

He glided the stemmed glass across the table to her, marveling to himself at the acuteness of her observation, especially considering all that this weary small girl, his baby, had been through today. Inwardly he shuddered. What soon *had* to be spoken, placed into words between them, couldn't be worse than his finding her on that roof, or their joint lying to Joanne, and yet he dreaded plunging on. His stomach, despite the liberal dosage of alcohol, still felt achingly hollow.

Daphne sipped, tasting the clear liquid slowly, carefully. Then she grimaced. "Do you really like this?"

"Don't you?"

"Oh, you. You're just making fun of me again. I bet you don't like it either."

He chuckled to himself, and then almost instantly felt a sharp pang. His dread was growing into something larger. Lurching an arm upward, he motioned for the check. The waiter nodded, and now Henry had no choice but to turn back to his child. Yes, no? Now, later? Go ahead, or wait perhaps until they got outside? How absurd, he thought, even asking himself these questions—and cowardly.

Steeling himself, he rested his forearms on the table, and leaned forward toward her.

"Daf, out on the fire escape, what did you see?"

She felt suddenly so afraid, more almost than out on that high fire-escape ladder.

"Whatever you remember, I'd like to know."

"Well, nothing much. I mean, most windows the shades were down."

"And me? You didn't see me?"

Saying no would be a lie. So she just shook her head.

"Then, on that roof, when I found you, you didn't *know* I was in there?"

"Well. See, I heard you. Your voice."

And that was the truth too!

Poor kid, he thought, it wasn't fair, hitting her with questions, putting her on the defensive. Yet if he could keep all this from Joanne for just one more week, just one, then he'd have some time and strength to cope, or at least try to cope. And it *could* be that Daf, despite her having been on that fire escape, did not really know. He would *have* to ask.

"Why didn't you knock on the window, tell me you were out there?"

"Oh, you know."

"*Do* I?"

"Daddy, she was naked."

53

The waiter put down the check. Henry stared at it numbly.

Outside it was hot.

Walking away from the Shanghai along upper Broadway, Daphne imagined she almost could be pushing her way through water or butter, the air felt so thick. A scrawny, Spanish-looking man wearing a pair of blue-and-yellow-striped shorts and nothing else, not even shoes, sauntered past. She looked up at her father, hoping he'd also think the man was funny-looking, and they'd exchange a smile. But Daddy's wide-open eyes didn't seem to be noticing her or the man.

"Thanks for taking me out. For such a good dinner."

"You're welcome."

He still hadn't smiled.

They ambled past stores, almost all of whose windows were veiled with metal grates: diamond-shaped ones, up-and-down crisscrossers, and some even were solid metal sheets, hiding everything.

Daphne's little toe felt pinched, and then it began to burn. She stopped.

Daddy kept walking.

"Wait up, will you!"

He stopped and turned.

"It's my dumb foot."

"Feel like a piggyback?"

"No."

He nonetheless swung an arm across her back, another under her knees, and in a twinkling had her hoisted and pinioned across his back and shoulders.

"Daddy, put me down!"

"Sh-h-h-h."

What was the use? She shut her eyes. The important thing was, when he left would he take her with him? What if he said no?

A breeze! Probably they'd rounded the corner, and begun heading down toward the river. She peeked. Yes, here it was darker. Not so many people would notice and stare.

They sat on a bench.

Henry gazed out at the Hudson. So damn serene, contrasted with the man-made hurly-burly on either side, flowing darkly, night and day, year after year, quietly, relentlessly, on and on, no matter who married, or divorced, or lied to their children, or deserted them.

"Dad"—no, not yet, she'd ask him something else—"why does this have to be a secret from Mom?"

"She'd probably get a little upset. And she's got those exams coming up. And her term papers. We wouldn't want to ruin all that for her."

"Oh."

"And me too. My play. There are just a few days of rehearsals left. It would be tough for me to concentrate on them if at the same time your mom, well, you know . . ."

"So then, after next week, it's not going to be a secret?"

"I don't like having a secret like this, Daf."

"But it's necessary?"

"Makes life a little easier, I guess, and a little harder."

Daphne belched. She felt nauseous. There was still the

awful question. But for now, maybe she'd better keep her mouth closed till her stomach settled.

"Daddy"—no, it was too hard to keep waiting—"when you go away, can I come too?"

"Darling, grownups, daddies and mommies, have to love one another. If they don't—and sometimes they try, but they can't—the best thing is for them to separate."

I don't believe you! But she'd only said it inside her head. She was afraid.

"Can you understand what I'm saying?"

"Yeah, I guess so."

More than once he had imagined this scene, trying to prepare for it, knowing it would be hard. But now he felt —anesthetized, as if he'd had to turn a switch, routing away all pain, all feeling.

"But, but," she stammered, "when you go, can I come too?"

"I can't promise you, sweetie. Because I don't know."

She dug her fingernails into the bench, hard.

"I think I'm going to catch cancer, and multiple sclerosis, and die."

"You're going to grow up and be very beautiful."

Grow up and this'll happen, grow up and that will, grow up, grow up, grow up, that's all they ever said. But when could you believe them? Because it had to take forever, even if maybe it *was* true.

Overhead she looked up at a tall tree. Its outstretched branch-arms seemed to tremble, then sway gracefully against the moonlight. Closing her eyes, listening to the soft rustling sounds, she imagined she'd become enveloped in a cozy cradle of limbs and leaves, rocking gently, high high above the world, up in that same tree. She could lean out over the edge and see her father below, tiny, all alone, turning his head, looking, wondering where that impossible Daphne could have disappeared to.

And then there right at the base of the trunk was that Mrs. Nyland. She was lying flat on her back, naked, but not on the ground. Encasing her was a coffin, with lots and lots of flowers arranged on both sides.

"Daf, this afternoon, you never did tell me why you came."

"Oh. Well, I wanted to ask what to get for your birthday."

He had started to rise from the bench.

"I suppose now you don't want me to get you anything anyway."

She saw him sink back down.

Shutting her eyes again, she flew back up into her tree.

Daphne lay there, letting her father tuck her in, just as if it were any plain old ordinary night. Through the quarter-open door, tat-tat, tat-tat-tat, she could hear Mom typing on and on, in spite of everything. Longings to hit, smash, scream, cascaded inside her head, throat, fingertips. All she actually did, though, was smile back up at him, pretending she believed him. Even though she knew everything was not going to be okay. How could it be? Then he bent to kiss her. She didn't kiss back. And he didn't ask her to. He stroked her head one more time, and went out.

In the dark she felt her face contort. She *had* to scream.

57

No, don't. Don't be an idiot. Twisting her whole body, she buried her face in the pillow. For a minute, an hour, she held her breath. Suddenly she flung off the covers, slid out of bed, and groped for something. Bumping into her baby rocking chair, she seized on her poor dear penguin, Oscar, who'd been sitting in it.

Wha-a-a-p! She was whacking him against the bedpost, the wall, again and again. Sss-s-s-sp! A huge rent appeared down his front. Pinnng! One of his plastic eyes popped off and clattered along the floor. Messes of cotton wadding were spewing and splattering out everywhere.

Suddenly the light was on. Vick had edged in and, wide-eyed, was watching her.

Though for an instant she felt blinded, she sustained her violent rhythm without a break. Quickly the stuffing was gone, and the toy animal became little more than a limp rag. Then she ripped off a leg, and flung it out the window.

"Hey, stop it, will you?"

She ignored him, and began tugging and wrenching at the other leg.

"Daffy, you crazy?"

It too got heaved out into the night.

He grabbed her hand. "Now come on."

"I hate her! Let go!"

"Stop it."

"I hate her!"

"Don't be an asshole."

Suddenly he felt a piercing in his arm. God, she was biting him!

Free of her brother's grasp, she hurled out the pathetic

remains of Oscar's shredded head and torso, and dove back onto her bed and burrowed beneath the rumpled blankets. She imagined the penguin falling, screaming and exploding into blood and dust and a little puff of steam.

Gingerly Vick approached. "Daf, what's going on?"

She pretended she couldn't hear.

"You okay?"

Her reply, though muffled by the bedclothes, was comprehensible. "Go away."

"You, uh, want an aspirin?"

"You don't know anything."

"Well, uh, we can't fix nothing if you don't tell me what it is." He waited. Then, near where he suspected her head was, he lifted the edge of the blanket a bit. "Well, can we?"

"I'm scared."

"I'll take care of you."

She didn't answer.

"Don't I always?"

Daphne poked her head out. "You won't tell anyone?"

Vick shook his head.

"Cross your heart?"

"And hope," he intoned very solemnly, "to die."

"But later"—she sat up—"don't you say crossing your heart is only for Catholics."

"Okay."

She clambered off the bed and poked her head out the door. No noise, except for the typing. Daddy, she decided, must have gone off to his dumb rehearsal. She shut the door, tested it, and glided back to her brother.

"Promise again."

"Jesus."

"Then just leave me alone."

"All right. I promise again."

"Well"—she hesitated, not at all sure how to begin— "you know when you went out before, with your baseball glove, for that tryout?" . . . and then it came, disjointedly at first, and then in a frenzied rush, everything: discovering the two of them through the window, sneaking on that bus and becoming Private Eye, and just now Daddy's admitting it all.

Vick's eyes dilated, his jaw sagged, and he sat heavily into the little chair at her chemistry table.

"And now any day"—she was fighting off tears as she finished—"he's leaving us."

"You sure? . . . I mean, you're not, well . . ." He was about to add, "imagining, making all this up." But right at his foot was a big piece of the penguin's insides, and he knew she would never have done that unless . . . He saw she had turned and pressed her face against the mattress. He felt kind of like crying too, but there had to be something better than that they could do.

"Well, then, we better talk to Daddy. Tell him we don't want him to go away."

"You promised!" And she swung about, as if poised to spring at him.

"Yeah, but . . . Say, did you ever think maybe he isn't really going away at all? Maybe he's just, what they call, laying her."

"What's that?"

"You know, it's when two people aren't married, and

they go away to a motel. Like what high school kids do in cars."

Grimly she shook her head. "No, he's just going to come on Sundays, once a month. And I bet we'll even have a Trinidad housekeeper" (Gloria had had that stringbean brown woman, Inez) "telling us what to do all the time, and hitting us."

For a long moment Vick thought. Then he sat alongside his sister. "Daf, Daddy told me. All that divorce stuff happened with the Blumenthals because they were neurotic."

"You calling me a liar?"

"No."

"'Cause he just told me, the best thing is for him and Mommy to get separate."

"He *said* that?"

"No"—she oozed sarcasm—"I'm making it up."

"Then, I guess . . . What about Mom? Maybe she could . . ." Looking into her doleful eyes, he let his voice trail off. "Yeah, I guess Mrs. Blumenthal never could do too much about it either, could she?"

He moved off, and nervously began plucking the pieces of cotton wadding off the floor. After a minute he'd collected them all and stood up. His sister, he saw, hadn't budged, as if she had nothing to do but wait for him to discover the perfect answer.

"For crying out loud, if we can't talk to Daddy or Mom, what's left? Bumping that lady off?"

"Oh, Vickie, do you think we could?"

He stared at her, not believing he'd heard right, and yet knowing he had.

"But could they send us to the electric chair?"

Dazed, he shook his head. Boy, could she come up with the weirdest stuff.

"They don't ever fry young kids, do they?"

"No, of course not. They just send you to reform school. And then when you get bigger, to jail for the rest of your life."

"It'd be worth it."

He heaved a big sigh. "Look, it's impossible anyway. She doesn't eat here, so you couldn't poison her. And where could *you* ever get a gun?"

"I'll find a way."

Stupid and impossible. He was positive. Still, the quiet way she'd said it had made him shiver, just a little.

CHAPTER 7

"This is it, kid."

He *had* remembered her. Bus drivers could too be nice.

"Thank you."

Holding onto the shiny metal pole, she stepped down, then had to let go as her foot dropped and finally touched the street. She scooted up to the sidewalk.

In front of her the building was white. Millions of little balconies, broad glassy picture windows, air-conditioning vents in rows under all of them. So much higher too than the houses on her street. And not jammed and crowded in. The marquee stretched for a mile, with shrubs bordering the whole walkway. She'd never seen an entrance set back so far from the sidewalk, and with two doormen at once. This had to be, she decided, where what they called millionaires lived.

Mrs. Nyland, might she be one? Why should she be? This isn't Sixty-eighth Street.

Four grownups who looked safe enough to ask passed along, and even two big kids who didn't seem tough, but then on the opposite corner Daf spotted a policeman.

"Four blocks, girlie, straight down, and then you make a left," and he pointed, showing which way left was.

"Thank you," and she began moving off.

"Hey!"

Unh . . . oh. Her heart sank. How did he know she hadn't gone back to school after lunch? Could they arrest you for that?

"You got your momma's permission to be out crossin' all them streets yourself?"

"Oh sure, officer. Of course I do."

He eyed her. She knew she had to stare right back, even though her stomach had begun to hurt, and she could feel tears welling up.

"All right, then don't forget, left is *that* way," and again he pointed.

The store windows along this avenue were wild. One had asparagus that had to be the biggest in the world. The stalks looked thick as cucumbers. Further along, she pressed her nose against a pane of plate glass, behind which a profusion of birthday candles, paper plates, party hats, thousands of them, were arranged in dazzling explosions of color: silver, orange, pink.

Turning off into the street, it felt so different. Quiet. No rumbling trucks. And green. Trees, right here in the city. Standing in little squares surrounded by sidewalk, they were smaller mostly than in Cedarhurst, but cute, with their fragile-looking branches, and polka dots of green leaves. Tiny low white wire fences framed the trunks. And inside the neat enclosed squares grew ivy and tulips, red at one tree, white at another, yellow. How weird, she thought, and pretty.

And the baby carriages! Two of them, huge, shiny black, glowing like mirrors or patent leather. Both were pushed by women in white uniforms. Nurses? They passed right close by, speaking strangely, probably a foreign language. Could they be agents pretending to be nurses? Why would baby carriages need nurses?

412, 416, 422. She darted quick looks at each building number she passed, but didn't stop or even slow down. Purposely she was staying on the even-number side. That way, when she reached 479, she'd be across the street. So she could get a view of the whole building, without twisting her neck, and people noticing. Daf also figured, here it'd be practically impossible accidentally to bump into that Mrs. Nyland.

There, by the very last house, 479. Fast, she swung her eyes back straight ahead, and walked on the few feet further to the fence at the end. Below, cars were streaking past. Just beyond the express highway was a river, the East River, because Miss Kornzweig once had shown the class a picture of the same tall smokestacks, where the electricity came from.

479 had a carved cement door frame which came to a point on top, like at a church, or a fortress. Daf's eyes roamed upward. No fire escapes. Were they in back? Or inside a courtyard? Her gaze dropped to the ground-floor windows. Grates with bars that looked thick as zoo cages guarded each of them. How could you *ever* get in there?

A delivery boy parked a bicycle, lifted out a carton from the basket, and went right in. So easy. So, go on! She tried smoothing her skirt. Dumb linen, she should never have worn it. Gets these awful wrinkles, always.

Well? Wait all afternoon, and today Mom really would let her have it.

No cars coming. She crossed. Funny—where was the doorman? The knob turned all right, but the door was heavy. She had to lean into it with all her strength to push it open.

Where were the rows of bells with names and apartment numbers next to them? No, the wall on the other side of the vestibule didn't have them either. Mailboxes would *have* to have apartment numbers, except they weren't here either. Ahead, leading into the lobby, were more doors, through which Daf couldn't see a thing. Curtains.

She looked around for an electric eye. Could be concealed. Well, so what if they spotted you on closed-circuit TV. As long as you really weren't stealing, what could they prove?

The next door opened more easily. Inside it was dark, like the basement in Cedarhurst, except the light here came in through two tall stained-glass windows, so it had faint red and blue glows. And so quiet. The carpet felt like it had to be a foot thick.

"Yes, Miss?"

She choked.

"Who're you lookin' for?"

Swallowing her gasp, she breathed. That voice didn't sound so bad really. Reminded her of someone on an old 4:30 movie, English, or Irish, or one of those.

Where? Casually she tried to peer around, but couldn't see him. That black alcove next to the front door, probably in there.

66

"Well?"

"See, uh, this girl in my class, she took home the wrong briefcase."

"What's 'er name?"

"Well, if I could look at the mailboxes, I'd see all the names you have here, and then I could remember."

"We don't have no mailboxes."

Run. She fought down the urge. Heck, on *International Secret Mission* they talked to invisible voices all the time.

"Is—is there someone here named Nyland?"

"What!" The voice chortled, then stopped. "She don't go to no school with you."

Light, sharp brightness, the door opening. A sloppy-haired, raggedy-dungarees girl about Daphne's age came in, pulling along a tall, graceful dog—a Borzoi, Daf thought.

Then Daf saw him. Yes, he *was* from that alcove, but shuffling out fast. No hat, scraggly white hair, and what looked like a black uniform, with his tie undone. Puffing a bit as he lumbered past Daf. She noticed he also had a huge red nose. He'd almost caught up with the dungarees girl, when he stopped and turned.

"Now I don' wan' to be findin' *you* here when I get back."

Daf slunk backward, then heard the elevator slam shut.

Hey, if he was an elevator man too, then he'd be gone for a while. Quick, she scooted to the little hall just beyond the elevator. Circling the room with her eyes, she found he had told the truth. No mailboxes.

A window, with a bench right under it. She clambered up on the bench, and pushed and tugged the window pulls. Finally it creaked, moved an inch, then more, enough so she could put her eyes to the crack. What a nice courtyard! More small trees, tiny hedges in picture-book arrangements. Craning and gazing upward, she saw there *was* a fire escape. Two fire escapes.

Whining distantly, whirring more closely, the elevator, she knew, would be back again any second. No time even to pull shut the window. Hopping down, running, rounding the corner out of the little hall, racing headlong across the dark lobby, wrenching at the inner door, which wouldn't open because in her haste she'd forgotten to turn the knob.

"Hey! You still here?"

She realized, turned it, flew through the vestibule, the outer door. Suddenly she was falling, feeling pain, a searing flame in her palms, her knees. "Aaaaaanh!" Her toe had caught on the outer sill, crashing her down on the brutal pavement. She cried. She didn't care who was watching, or how awful she looked. It hurt too much.

Strong hands, and gentle ones, she felt, were picking her up.

"Hurt baid?"

A Black man, she thought, but he wasn't. His beard tickled her nose. She could hardly see his face, his beard and hair were so thick and red.

"You okay?"

Even though her knee still felt like it was on fire, she nodded.

She saw him pull something from one of his pockets and offer it to her. A licorice stick.

"Chew on this. Best remedy known to man for scraped

68

knees, runny noses, and pimples where you don't want 'em."

Everything was too surprising.

The man, who looked like a giant hippy cowboy, had gotten back up, and was sponging a long, thin paper strip to the cement at one side of the door. Sssssssssp, he pealed the paper back off, and there, as if growing out of the pavement, was a jack-in-the-beanstalk, six-foot-high daisy painted right on the concrete. Daf saw another one already on the other side. Up around the top, he began sponging on little stickers, letters, which would have to spell things. What? Fascinated, forgetting her throbbing kneecap, she followed his every move. He paused, examining his work. In orange and purple, she saw he had spelled out, L-O-V-E R-A-C-H-E-L.

People, Daf noticed, were collecting and watching: two little boys absent-mindedly spinning Yo-yos, the doorman from across the street, a Good Humor bicycleman, a colored woman with a flowered hat.

Marching toward them came a fat lady in tight yellow pants. Even before she'd said a word, just from the way her breath was heaving, Daf knew she was angry.

"What is going on here?"

The cowboy man, not looking worried at all, beamed a big smile at her. "Sonny-James Parker, ma'am. Pleased to make your acquaintance. And this here's whut the young folks nowadays call a love offerin'."

"Does the management," her voice getting shriller, "know about this?"

He seemed puzzled. "Is it, you don't like love offerin's, or you jes don' like this here one?"

"Listen, kook," now she was yelling, "you better get away from here!"

He extended his hand toward her. She quickly stepped back, her peroxide hair and fleshy legs quivering, scared. All he did, though, was offer her a licorice stick.

"No hard feelin's."

"I'm warning you," she growled.

Smiling still, he pulled something out of his other pocket. "Hey, some chicken corn?"

The woman, boiling, about-faced, and swiftly waddled off into the house.

He slapped his thigh, chuckling, and then flung the handful of candy bits high in the air, letting them hail down over everyone.

Daphne, in spite of her soreness and her worry about losing Daddy, laughed too. This Sonny-James made it all so funny.

Suddenly the door swung back, and the old doorman, tightening up his tie, and wearing his cap now, stepped out, blinking in the light. He stared at the cluster of people for a second, and then turned and gaped at the "art work."

"What kinda wise guy . . ." He shook a fist at Sonny-James. "There's laws against defacin' private property, an' I aim to see them obeyed!" He motioned toward the door. "Now you get in here and wait for the cops, and then we'll see what's so damn funny!"

"Oh, man." Cowboy shook his head pityingly. "Don't you know this here's official municipal business, for the deputy commissioner of beautification?"

"Oh, yeah?"

The uniformed attendant's eyes, despite his strong, belligerent tone, had clouded just a bit. He was pretty damn sure this woolly-headed freak was lying. But with the whole city psycho already, wog garbagemen going off on strike, the mayor turning Madison Avenue into a silly-ass promenade, next thing probably you'd have goofball here and his spic mistress moving in as tenants. So what the hell could you ever really be sure about any more?

But another look at the cockamamie's psychedelic pastels, coupled with a vision of the landlord chewing him out, firing him even, as that young punk bastard had more than once threatened—and the old doorman made up his mind, wheeled about, and began heading for the phone.

"Hey, now wait!"

Should he?

"You ain't even ast to see my *official* I.D."

Sonny-James pulled out a billfold and rifled through it, looking surprised and then pained that he couldn't seem to find that I.D. Again he reached down into his pocket.

"No, don't imagine you'd accept this here, would you?"

He had pulled out a licorice stick.

The doorman looked numb.

Sonny-James took a bite out of the licorice, and chewed with obvious relish.

"Say, how about my official gun? Would that prove it to ya?"

"Hunh?"

He pulled one out.

Daphne's tongue and mouth glued together.

The doorman, cowering, held his shaking hands half up. "Jesus, don't shoot. Now, please. For the love of God . . ."

Suddenly a stream of water splashed off his red nose, and began dripping off his frozen chin, down onto his tie, shirt, uniform.

Daf exhaled. A water pistol, boy.

A fresh stream splattered on the yellow-pants lady, who'd come out and stood behind the doorman.

"Aaaaaannngh!"

"You piddly punk!" The doorman's voice had finally come back. "You half-assed overgrown Communist freak! I'll get the cops on you, so help me. And I'll prefer charges meself!" He skittered back in.

The onlookers, Daphne saw, were all smiling. Cowboy man, shaking his head, was laughing softly, and she began to chuckle too.

"Come on, pussy willow." He held out a hand to her. "We better move."

Should she? Why not? Being with him, maybe she wouldn't have to feel scared.

They ran.

Higher, higher, on the next push he gave her, or maybe the one after that, her swing would soar off into the clouds or moon, and she'd be safe forever.

She looked down. The whole world was a whirry, happy playground.

Sonny-James Parker, maybe *that's* why he was so magical, because he had kind of a make-believe name.

They were ambling to a bench.

72

"Daf, you live in that there building?" And he pointed back toward where they'd first met.

"No, un-unh."

He looked surprised.

"Then, uh, who you know who does?"

Why was he asking this?

She shrugged, "No one, really."

"Oh."

Why'd he seem disappointed? His love offering? That name he'd been pasting up, Rachel?

Sitting next to him and licking an orange popsicle, she had a great idea, because he looked so strong.

"Sonny-James, did you ever kill anybody?"

"Hell, no."

He got up. Was he going away? Or just to the trash can to throw away the wrappers? Yes, oh thank God.

"But what if they were doing something real bad?"

"Like what?"

"Like—like taking away all your toys."

"That's serious, all right. But I don't believe it's whut they call a hangin' crime."

"Okay. Then . . . what if they were going to burn your house down?"

His forehead crinkled.

"Why'd anyone be fixin' to burn down *your* house?"

She could tell he didn't believe it, but then maybe he was right, and nothing really would happen, because . . .

"Look, if I promise not to kill anybody, and then my house does burn, will you be my daddy?"

She imagined the campfire, even smelled the smoke. Their two horses tied up to a tree nearby would be grazing, whinnying. He'd play a guitar, singing very softly. She'd be making coffee, or hunter's stew, and serving it to him, and he'd taste it, and say, "Fantastic. You are one great kid." She'd be dressed in cowboy clothes too, and even have her own gun, a little pistol, in case of rattlesnakes. And there'd be a gorgeous pink sunset, with mountain peaks. But that wouldn't be the end. Because the next day they'd go riding on and on, always together.

Walking out of the playground, he was holding her hand.

"Daf, din't you tell me you got a daddy, a pretty fine one?"

At the curb she looked down at a beer can, twistedly squashed. "But—if something happens to him."

"You are a worry-busy, know that? Daf, your house ain't gonna burn."

The bus, she saw, would be pulling up any second.

He wouldn't help. Probably he'd just ask more questions and make her give away all the secrets, and then tell on her. Sure, he looked magical, and he did stuff that made him seem kind of magical, but for it to be real, probably he had to be on TV. And this sure wasn't TV.

The bus screeched to a halt.

No one else was waiting. She climbed up.

He called "G'bye!" and waved.

She didn't answer. What was the good?

CHAPTER 8

The elevator door opened.

Vick, instead of going in, sidled off toward the marble bench against the lobby wall. He was nibbling at his lip. Why did thinking of a good lie have to be so hard? Daf never had trouble. She'd have five different ones in a minute, all good too. Sitting, he touched the areas around his nose, pressing lightly to try and pinpoint his bruises. Hell! The tenderness, he discovered, was on both sides. Probably he had *two* black eyes.

Think, think, think, or Mom could just decide he shouldn't play baseball any more, for a month, forever. Just because of one dumb fight that had nothing to do with baseball really. He drummed his fingers on the stone seat. If he told her it was the ball, or bat, or he'd been hit running, or sliding, she'd say something like, That game's too dangerous, you're too young, wait till you get bigger. And if he told what really happened, how those Spanish kids could start punching you for no reason, she might never let him go to that park any more. Might even take his glove away. He sighed and slowly got up. It was hopeless.

Unless, maybe, he could get her talking about something real fast, so she wouldn't even notice his eyes. But what? He pressed the elevator button. For instance, what about this girl friend Daddy was supposed to have, or divorce? Those were things any grownup was supposed to be interested in. Maybe even all that stuff Daf was babbling about, like Daddy's going away, he could find out if anything like that really ever could happen.

She opened the door.

"Hi, Mom."

"My, you're home early."

Head bowed, he tried to edge by.

"Vickie, your forehead looks scratched. What happened? Is that a black eye?"

She towed him into the kitchen, over near the window.

"Oh, you poor baby. Does it hurt?"

"A little."

She swabbed him with a warmly moistened dish towel.

He wanted her to stop so he could get out before she started with the questions, but her fussing did feel sort of nice, soothing. So maybe if he let her stay busy fixing him up, she never would ask.

"That eye needs some ice."

She wrapped the cubes in another dish towel, and held the compress below his eye. The pain melted into numbness.

"I've never seen anything so hideous, ghoulish almost. Except once." Then she launched into how he'd fallen out of his baby carriage, with the nine stitches, and no nurse or doctor to be found in that hospital emergency room, and Vick knew he could relax. Once she got going

76

on one of her stories, she wouldn't ask about him, or his eyes, or anything.

"Would you come keep me company while I do the grocery shopping?"

That probably meant now he was safe. No more real chance of her taking away his glove, or forbidding Riverside Park. So then, why didn't he feel more glad?

They rounded the corner past the tiers of beer and soda, and were approaching the dairy counter.

"Go over and pick me out two-dozen eggs. But open them first. Be careful what you get, you understand?"

One egg in the first carton he tried had a cracked, poked-in end. The second box smelled funny. Looking closely, he saw greenish mold spots on the cardboard. A foul, rotten odor crept up his nostrils. Uuuugh. Quickly he slapped it back down. Finally two okay ones. Limping slightly, he rejoined his mother, who was bending over the meat counter, picking up the topmost packages to see if choicer or less fatty-looking cuts lay beneath. He nestled the eggs into the cart between an oversized box of detergent and a firm cabbage. She was watching, he saw, so he made sure to wedge the pickle jar in next to the eggs too. That way they never could get jostled loose.

His eye had started to throb again. Daphne's nutty talk about killing, for some reason, came back to him.

"Mom, you think we could ever move back to Cedarhurst?"

Had she heard him?

"How's that eye feel now?"

"Not too bad."

77

She picked out a small roast and a packet of hamburg.

"Why"—she shook her head disapprovingly—"do you always have to get involved in these things?"

Boy, she sure could be dumb about fights.

They rounded another corner and began the frozen vegetables. Down the aisle toward the cash registers, he heard loud voices. People, he saw, were standing still, turning in that direction.

"Let me see what that is," and he moved off, and then wove his way through the check-out crowd.

A woman was yelling, "Wadda you mean, you no take-a my check! You take-a evybody check. You take-a da welfare. You take-a da food stamps. I work! My husban-a work! So wadda you mean, you no take! You wan' I no eat? You wan' I die!"

Vick couldn't hear what the manager was saying back, but he could see the white-aproned man ingratiatingly smiling, nodding, lips constantly working, while he tugged the seething woman off with him.

Vick again thought of his sister. Her raving about dying, killing. Why had Daf not met him today after school?

His mother was poking through the frozen-juice cans.

"Mom, why do people get divorced?"

Joanne, peering at a smudged-ink price stamp, was having trouble discerning whether the large-sized Sunkist, supposedly on special today, really was cheaper than two of the small Birds Eye.

"What?"

"Divorce, is it really bad?"

Joanne at the same time had been listening in her mind

for the tenth or twentieth time to Professor Albrecht's comment on her "Marivaux in Germany." "Brilliant, Mrs. Beckman. Best paper zis year. But you must footnote ze whole Mannheim connection, no? Und zen we submit to ze journal, no?" Her chest swelled, glowed, even here, behind a supermarket cart. Joanne Beckman appearing in *The Franco-German Comparative Literature Quarterly.* It could mean a full-time faculty appointment even before she'd completed her doctorate.

Then hearing, looking at her bruised son, suddenly she felt the icy coldness of the cans she was holding.

"Why do you ask?"

"Oh, just thinking, I guess."

Her expression darkened. She absently lowered all the containers she'd been examining into the wagon, her eyes remaining fixed on him.

Vick, surprised, felt like kicking himself. Idiot. Why couldn't he have asked something plain, like, What're we having for supper?

"Vick, I'm waiting."

"Well, the Blumenthals."

"But, that was last summer. Why bring them up now? Here?"

He shrugged, and got very busy reading frozen pizza labels. He had to get out of this. How? Some story? All right, what if he told what Daf had said? Everything? . . .

He pointed to the stack of frozen cheesecakes. "Could we get one?"

"Why suddenly are you so interested in the Blumenthals' divorce?"

"I—I don't know."

79

She snatched up the aluminum-foil cake container and dropped it into the wagon.

"What," he mumbled, "are we having for supper?"

"Why are you changing the subject?"

Her voice, knifelike now, was stabbing into him.

"Can I go home? My eye's starting to hurt again."

"Answer me, Vick."

"Please?"

He started to move off. She grabbed his arm.

Her Vick, so strangely jumpy, spitting out a question like divorce, and then running away. Why? But couldn't it just as easily have been something at school, or between kids on the street? Why assume it had to do with Henry? But then, why else would the boy be so uptight?

"Vick, whatever it is you've seen, heard, know about, you've *got to tell me.*"

He shut his eyes. Her words were needles. Pricking everywhere. This must mean, he thought, Daf is right. Mom in a million years would never hiss at him, here, in the middle of Bohack's, unless this divorce stuff really was . . .

"Well?"

"I don't know. See, Daf said something the other day about Gloria. Besides, I didn't feel like talking about groceries all the time, or my black eye, or . . ."

Joanne, becoming aware again, *seeing* his bruises, swollen, discolored skin, felt a rush of remorse. She released his arm.

Vick decided now he'd better stay.

Above the frozen-food bin, he looked up at an array of hardware items, hung on little racks, in see-through packets. His gaze drifted past measuring spoons, ice cream scoops, to a set of steak knives.

Henry. Joanne pushed and jostled the rickety shopping cart over the grating pavement. Yes, him, this *had* to do with him. He must have let something slip. A complaint about her? God knows, he did that all the time. Or maybe a question, theoretical of course. "What would you kids think of . . . my living somewhere else? Our moving out together and leaving your mother?"

But no point in dragging it out of Vick, with that eye. Let him be. Bring this to Henry. Next week maybe. Definitely. She'd write it on the kitchen calendar, so she couldn't possibly forget. And this time she *would* do it. Joanne could feel tears starting to come, and blinked rapidly to hold them back.

CHAPTER 9

Daphne took a quick look, and then switched the channel. And again. And twice more. Crumb, *Rawsmoke* was the only decent show on. She flicked off the TV.

Vick, who was Scotch-taping baseball-player clippings into his scrapbook, looked up, surprised.

"What's wrong with *Rawsmoke?*"

"Nothing."

"So why'd you turn it off?"

"I don't know."

She had to have *some* reason. Looking at her, he waited.

"Well," she blurted, impatient for him to stop staring, "cowboys are all phonies anyway."

Boy, was she for real? She always loved those big gunslingers. Suddenly they're phonies? He saw her stretch out on the rug and shut her eyes. Yeeeah, ever since he'd come back from Bohack's with Mom, and found Daf waiting for them, she'd been strange. Not screaming-and-yelling strange, though, like yesterday. Just funny quiet stuff. At dinner eating those vegetables she usually never touched, not saying a word about his black eye. Now this queer, fast shutting off the TV.

Actually he'd been waiting for a good time to talk

about Mom, 'cause of the supermarket. On and off he'd been wondering, sort of, if maybe there *was* something they ought to try and do about this divorce stuff. But what?

He saw her get up and start to leave.

"Where you going?"

"I need some paper."

"You got a whole white pad there."

"I want some of Daddy's."

"What for?"

"Because it's his, that's what for!"

She left.

No, Daf sure wasn't much for talking, not today. Boy, in this kind of mood, she might even start in again with that scary mouthing-off of hers.

Daphne, gliding along the hall, paused outside Mom's door. Tat-tat, tat, tat-tat-tat. Mom wouldn't come out of there probably for hours. No danger.

Slipping into the front-hall closet, holding her breath, Daf closed the door behind her. Dark, black. What if there were rats crawling out of the floor, or the moldings, or the clothes? Her anxious, probing fingers felt the light switch finally, and pressed-pushed it up.

No rats. But there, sure enough, bulging-looking in the corner, Daddy's briefcase. She crouched, fumbled with the catch, got it to release, then spread the case open. Red cardboard legal folders stuffed it full. Up against one side, though, should be yellow pads. 'Cause he always carried them. Yes, but only one, though. She hesitated, then pulled it out. Something else caught her eye, new, never in there before. Jammed between two of the reddish containers, a gray wallet-sized leatherette folder. She maneuvered it out. Gold-stamped writing said, BERKEY PRESTIGE PRINTS. She flipped the smallish folder open. Her? Daf snapped shut her eyes. No, it couldn't be. Gritting her teeth, she looked again. Yup, under the clear plastic, that same one all right, only this time in a bathing suit. A nauseous sour taste crept from Daphne's stomach up into her mouth.

When she stole back in, Vick, she saw, was still scissoring up the sports pages. The TV was off still too. She flicked it back on, then shoved his lopsided hassock against the door.

"Whatcha doing that for?"

"You'll see."

He waited a long minute for her to explain, then shrugged and turned back down to Yastrzemski grinning, just after he'd swatted a center-field home run. In color, from *Sports Illustrated*, Yaz was going to get pasted all by himself on one whole page of the scrapbook. Suddenly stuck over Yaz, he saw a woman in a bathing suit sitting on a rock. What was Daf doing?

"Guess who?"

Loudish shooting was crackling out of the TV, and he wasn't sure he'd even heard her right.

"Hunh?"

"That's her."

"Who?"

"*You know.*"

He bent from his sister's eerily glowing eyes back to the snapshot. The woman's bathing suit, he noticed, was

85

black, one piece. Her body looked young, springy, slim, and with long hair down her back.

"All right, so you got a picture of some woman at the beach. So what?"

"She was in Daddy's briefcase."

"Oh."

The achey throbbing in his eye came back. Hell, there could be other explanations for this, all kinds of explanations.

"Okay, maybe Daddy's just keeping it there for something legal, say, evidence for one of his cases."

Daphne slowly, grimly, shook her head.

"Un-unh. She's the exact same one."

Vick, impelled by a new curiosity, reached for the folder.

"Careful!" She grabbed his wrist. "Finger marks. Don't get it all sloppy."

Vick held it close, inches from his eyes. Her hair, that seemed more interesting. Why? . . . Sure, Mom always wore a bathing cap. This lady let her long blond hair get wet. Looked so relaxed, cool. Well, if they were going to be stuck with some new stepmother, at least she had nice hair.

"I bet," Daf ferociously asserted, *"she's* even why we moved here."

Vick, peering down into the dark street where they weren't allowed this late, thought that was crazy.

"You didn't ever believe that stuff about coming here for cultural advantages, did you?"

Why worry now *why* they'd moved here. It was too late.

"You know, you never got a black eye that bad back in Cedarhurst."

Daf *had* noticed. Inwardly he smiled.

"It's *her* fault, all right. It's got to be."

Did Daf know even more stuff?

"What makes you so positive?"

"'Cause they don't give you those bathing-suit pictures unless—unless she meant to, take him away forever . . . But we won't let her."

"What could we ever do?"

"Plenty."

"Aw, Daf, you better stop this big talk. The only way we could ever get rid of anybody is if you were Superman for a day. Carry her off to the moon. Or maybe, if you're a little tired, just fly her out to the middle of the ocean and drop her."

"Geez, if we only could."

"Only you're *not* Superman."

It got quiet then except for the TV, and he turned back to centering Yastrzemski on the blank page.

"I know a way," she said, almost whispering. "And nobody has to be Superman either."

What could she be thinking of? Not that she'd ever do it, of course.

Funny. Why was she pushing the hassock away from the door, and sticking her head out into the hallway?

"It's okay," she murmured. "Come on."

"Hunh? Where?"

"Up to the roof."

"Now?"

"Vick, please?"

87

He made a face. "Look, I'll turn the TV louder. Then who could ever hear you?"

"Forget it."

The slow way she turned her head away, and then picked up the yellow pad, he knew she meant it.

They tiptoed along the foyer, she first. At the closet, she poked him.

"You be lookout."

He watched her crouch and tuck the leatherette folder back into Daddy's briefcase.

While she clicked shut the front door, he held his breath, then shook his head admiringly. How quietly she'd managed it.

Half a flight up, at the landing, he whispered, "She is pretty."

"So what?"

The rest of the way, no one talked.

Breezes hit her face and blew through her hair, as soon as they stepped out onto the roof. At least it was cooler than last night. At the edge she jimmied herself up on her elbows, and looked down at the specks of light cruising the street. Under the street lamps, circular sections of car roofs glowed. People flitting along the sidewalk were faint tiny shadows.

"Look!"

Her brother's finger was pointing across the alley to a window in the top floor of the next building. A heavy, hairy man—she could see only his top half, which didn't have any clothes on—was on a bed, kneeling sort of. A woman lay under him, and he was kissing her—her face, her shoulder, her arm, all over. The woman was slim, breasts which didn't sag at all, a little pretty even. How could she like having that fat man slobber over her? But she *was* smiling, then puckering and kissing him right back. The man's head rolled and faced out the window. Did he see them? Suddenly he moved, disappeared, and next it all went black.

"I guess"—Vick sounded wistful—"they put the light out."

"I'm glad. It was disgusting."

Besides, if they stayed up here too long, Mom might find they were missing. She pulled at his arm, and they both sat, backs resting against the brick. Before, while climbing up here, she'd prepared sort of in her mind how to say stuff, and not just how you could sneak into that building, but even about Sonny-James too. Now, though, no words were coming.

"Daf"—Vick broke the silence—"I looked it up in the encyclopedia. Divorce."

"So?"

"There's like a million every year—maybe two, three million, and it doesn't say a thing about anybody being —gotten rid of."

"You want to hear how we could do it, or don't you?"

He wasn't answering. Probably he did not want to hear.

"All right, sure."

Should she tell? He was only asking because he was nosey, not really to help. It was hopeless. She ought to go to sleep and die. Or she could jump off this roof. Or maybe they'd both get sent to an orphanage and sleep in a huge hospital room with forty beds.

"Well?"

Was she wrong about him? New, madly leaping hope began exploding inside her.

"See, the place has a doorman. But he's real old. Also he runs the elevator. So it's easy to get past him. So then all we do is come down the fire escape, turn on her gas, and seal up the window with Saran Wrap. And then I bet you a million dollars we move back to Cedarhurst."

Vick rose. He felt like tear-assing back to his room. Instead, though, he looked off toward where the kissing fat man had been. He wished Daffy was somewhere way over there now too.

"So what do you think?"

She, he saw, had risen too.

"Well, what if there is no gas, only electric?"

"Oh, silly, apartments always have gas. Electric's only for houses."

Boy, did she believe that?

"It's true!"

"Then what if"—there had to be a million reasons why it could never work—"if the fire escape's in this lady's bedroom, and she wakes up?"

"Well . . . we could slip her a knockout pill. In the restaurant where she eats."

Geez, what was the use? If he said, They'd never find the restaurant where she eats, or never be able to get in there, or never get close to her table, Daf would dream up some other screwball plan and pitch it at him.

"Look, so Daddy has her picture. Lots of people carry around pictures. That doesn't prove he's going away with her."

"You chicken?"

"For crying out loud! Did you ever see a single program where the crooks didn't get caught?"

"Then how come they never caught the crook who stole Grandma Edna's silver, and her mink stole?"

"Listen, you know what they do with the ones they *don't* catch? It's just as bad for them, 'cause it's *their* pictures that get stuck up in the post office."

"So big deal."

"So big deal yourself. Only I don't feel like getting sent to any reform school, where they beat you with rubber hoses."

"And I'm not going to let *her* take Daddy away!"

Her body shook, and she was crying. She tried to stop, but the trouble wasn't just her eyes. The spasms began way down in her throat, or her stomach. As fast as the tears dribbled out, she wiped them away, but that didn't help much. Suddenly she wished she could kill Vick too. But that didn't matter either, because now she'd do everything herself. Only instead of that Mrs. Nyland getting killed, it wouldn't work, and she, Daphne, would fall off that fire escape. And it would serve them all right.

"Daf, stop," he pleaded. "Don't cry, will you?"

"What do *you* care?"

He hated it when she cried.

"Hey, Daf"—he strained to sound gentle, and hopeful—"maybe I have an idea."

She didn't believe him. Still, she blew her nose.

"Look, what if we go over there, ring the bell, and tell this lady who we are . . ."

"And she'll call Daddy."

"We'll ask if she's really going to do it."

"She is!"

"She'll laugh probably. And then she'll say, What a crazy idea."

"Yeah?" Her spasms subsided, and her tears. "And if she says she *is* going to?"

"Well"—Vick began to feel trapped—"we'll ask her not to."

"And when she still says no?"

"Well . . ."

"Well?"

Vick's vaguely trapped feeling grew huge, doors closing, brick walls closing in on him. What if that woman *did* say she was going to take Daddy away? If Daf were right? *What* would he do?

"Then, I guess, we'll have to see."

She thrust forth her hand.

Vick had no choice. He had to take it.

Solemnly they shook.

CHAPTER 10

Daf had intended to ask at breakfast, or maybe right after. But all day there had been perfect reasons, kind of, why it seemed better to wait just a *few* more minutes. Mom, Daf had kept telling herself, would positively say yes. 'Cause what could be so terrible about allowing them to go fly kites in the park first thing tomorrow morning? After lunch, though, at Daf's first real try, Mom had been reading and taking notes, a deadly time to interrupt. The next sally Daf ventured from her room, Mom, cleaning the chicken with a butcher knife, had shushed her. Then, soon as Mom had slid the baking dish into the oven, she'd disappeared to wash her hair.

Sitting down for dinner, Daf had sworn and crossed her heart she was going to ask, definitely, not one bit more shilly-shallying, and *before* people finished the chicken. Now, though, they were having such a good time, Daddy right here telling a story, Mom giggling, everyone eating a real chicken, not some dumb TV dinner, it seemed wrong. Like, maybe sneaking up to that woman's apartment *was* weirdo, and Vick was right. And if Daf dared lie, even a harmless little nothing lie, all this niceness might turn nasty and rotten.

"Daffy, listen, you'll get a kick out of this."

93

"I'm listening."

"So then this actress, talk about crazy, she rips open" —Henry twisted his mouth and at the same time made grotesque hand gestures mimicking the woman—"rips open a box of dried cereal, Rice Krispies, and she's flinging them, whole handfuls, in the director's face, in his hair, all over the stage!"

Daf watched everyone start laughing, then quickly forced herself to join in too. The story didn't seem funny to her, but then she'd heard only half. Mom was keeping on chortling. Boy, for a change, was she ever in a great mood! Now maybe . . . ?

"Mom, tomorrow can Vick and I go out, very early, and fly our kites in the park?"

"Hey, can I come along too?" Daddy asked, suddenly, as if it were the simplest thing in the world.

For an instant Daphne froze, then pressed her lips into a smile. Why didn't Vick say something? Her brother, though, just scooped up another forkful of mashed potatoes and plunged it into his mouth, as if the only thing in the world going on was eating. Daf racked her brain to think of something, fast. Well, they'd just have to do it some other day, unless . . .

"Sure. Great. But you have to get up early, eight o'clock, so we can get out there before that field gets all crowded."

"On second thought," Henry snorted softly, and shook his head, "I better take a rain check. After the rehearsal we're probably going to have tonight, there's like no chance I could make it up that early. I'll be lucky if I'm back *here* by eight o'clock."

Her mother's brow, Daf saw, furrowed deeply.

"Is that okay with you, Mom?"

"Your father"—her voice had turned sharp and sour again—"seems already to have given you his okay, without bothering to consult me."

Daf stuffed her mouth with potatoes too, so no one could see her smile.

For a long time it had been hard to sleep. Almost regularly now, Daf would check the clock, the window, to see how light it was getting to be, and then snuggle face down into the crinkly softness of her pillow to shut out how they could get knifed on the way over, or how that doorman might lock them in a secret storage room. This time she crawled under the sheet and blanket, her head too, and pretended they were a fortress. Even atom bombs couldn't get through. Also, she fired off a rare counter-radar machine that steered away the bombs. Then, squirming out for air, she again tried to sleep, and forget, at least until the alarm rang. But after a minute, creatures from outer space descended shooting invisible rays, and she had to duck under and steer them away too.

When hordes of screaming Viet Cong began storming her bunker, she got up. Next probably it'd be Nazis or Chinese Communists, so what was the use? Quarter after five, the clock read. She reached over and pushed in the alarm. Still a whole hour—an hour and a quarter really. Zero-hour wake-up wasn't until six-thirty. At least, though, it wasn't pitch-dark any more. Down in the empty street, the clusters of waiting garbage cans stood out clearly. Now even muggers had to be sleeping.

95

In the bathroom she stopped herself just as she was about to flush the toilet.

Geez, what to wear? Yesterday afternoon she'd been in front of the mirror for hours, narrowing her choices finally to two: the solid cranberry and the red-and-navy check. The cranberry with its full gathered skirt made her look fluffier, cuter, but the check was more serious, grownup—businesslike. Vick had liked the check. It was more, he'd said, what Mom would wear, and Daf had agreed. Now she wasn't sure. The big pink flowers appliquéd on the cranberry *were* awfully happy-looking. Maybe, though, that would be the best, or would it?

Waiting for the slowpoke clock to move, she picked up her *Golden Book of Chemistry Experiments.* The ammonia fountain, with the liquid turning pink and shooting upward, looked spectacular in the illustration. But figuring how you did it, reading the long words, phenolphthalein, was an impossible blur. Especially when every other minute her eyes kept drifting away to the clock.

Six-thirty. Finally. With both dresses folded over her arm, she tiptoed into Vick's room, crouched, and whispered directly into his ear, "Vick? Vick, hey, Vick."

Groggily his body shifted.

"Wake up, will you?"

He opened bleary eyes.

She held up the dresses, displaying one with each hand. "Which? This, or this?"

"Oh, come on," he moaned. "Didn't we do all that yesterday?"

"Seriously," she insisted, "will you?"

96

He rose on an elbow, and scratched his head. "I got an idea."

"Hunh?"

"Maybe none of those are right."

"Why not?"

"'Cause, well, maybe this woman'll listen to us more if we looked underprivileged."

"Black or Puerto Rican?"

"No, no, no, no. Just, well, poor."

"Like—rags?"

"Well, like old, faded maybe, and worn-out."

"What good would that do?"

"Make her feel sorry for us. You know, like beggars."

"Yeah, but she knows Daddy. So how could we be beggars?"

Vick stretched. Probably it wouldn't make one difference what they wore.

"Besides, those kind of clothes make you feel awful inside." Then suddenly Daf knew he *had* to be wrong. "That's a fancy building. Not like this. With a doorman."

"So?"

"So if you're an underprivileged beggar, you don't belong. They don't ever let you in."

Waiting for the crosstown, forgetting how delighted she'd been with Vick finally for preferring her cranberry, Daf grew impatient, jumpy. She began nurturing little buds of anger. Here they'd been waiting and waiting, and now no more buses would ever come. And it would be all his fault. He had *had* to finish two bowls of dried cereal. He had *had* to waste thirty-nine hours scrounging

97

after a hiding place for their kites. So what if someone found them and swiped them. Couldn't you always say they'd got stuck in a tree, or got broke landing, or something?

A bus. Finally. That very instant the angry lump clotting her throat dissolved. Suddenly she felt so grateful he was coming with her, and helping, she had an urge to hug him. And he looked handsome too, in his blazer with the gold buttons, hair combed. You hardly even noticed his reddish-blue-ish eye.

As the bus neared the park, Vick, eyes glued to the window, envying, watched the kids with their bats and gloves loping along to their ball game. A new thought came, obliterating his envy.

"What if the doorman buzzes up to her, and she says, no, she don't want us to come up?"

"Who's talking to the doorman? We're going in with someone—like we belong there."

He blinked. Man, she'd fired that back fast—like lightning. His lips spread into a slight smile, admiring, impressed.

On the naked lady's tree-lined block, they passed a boy and girl intently spinning Yo-yos. Daf, slowing down, looked back at them over her shoulder. The girl was a whiz, looping hers straight out, dead man's float, short hops, long hops. Daf imagined herself on TV, a Sunday-morning kids' show, Yo-yo contest, the finals . . .

"Come on"—Vick tugged at her—"or your girl-friend lady could be gone shopping by the time we ever get up there."

"It's Sunday."

At the borderline, where the next-door house ended and hers began, Daphne, putting out her hand, stopped him.

"Here?"

She pointed ahead to the churchlike doorway, which still was faintly decked with Sonny-James' giant cockamamies.

Intrigued, he whistled silently.

They waited, leaning against a shiny parked car.

"We better get busy, do something," she murmured anxiously, "so nobody'll see we don't belong."

He drifted off to the front of the car. Queer hood decoration.

"Hey, this is a Bentley. That's English."

"Shhhhhhh!"

The man coming toward them looked perfect. Old. So old his Sunday paper kind of bent him forward, like it was too heavy for him. As he came close, Daf, fascinated by his flouncy silk tie and cute white flower in his lapel, had to force herself not to stare. Then she noticed he was humming to himself, dreamily. The second he'd passed, she, a finger to her lips, yanked Vick's hand and nodded to him. The two children, after one scary fumbling moment, fell into place directly behind the elegant oldster, looking to all the world as if they were his own grandchildren.

In the elevator going up, Daphne kept her eyes on the floor. The doorman hadn't said anything yet, but he still could. Would he? She couldn't resist darting a look at him. His eyes, sure enough, were aimed right at her,

99

his forehead crinkled, probably with trying to recognize, remember. Thank God, then, he had to get busy stopping the car, and sliding open the door.

Bzzzzzzzzz! Rachel froze. What in Christ is this? The doorbell, without a prior call up from the lobby, is *not* supposed to ring. And sure as hell, not the first thing Sunday morning. No doorman today? Out on Social Security is where he *ought* to be. So, who? Henry? No, he'd call first. Sonny-James going wild again? Unless it's a mistake, and after a minute, mystery man'll just go away.

Bzzzzzzzzz! Sonny, it had to be. She smiled, touched, despite the goddamned nuisance. Should she see him, try to explain, firmly? She folded and put down a chunk of newspaper—she'd been scanning the auction ads in the classified—rose from her burnished Empire settee, retied the belt on her robe, and walked softly to the door. Before flipping the peephole, she checked the latch. Could those be children? Yes, a boy and a girl. Nicely dressed, though, and white. From here in the building maybe, selling raffles or something?

"Yes?"

"Uh . . ." Daf's voice dribbled away.

"Could we"—Vick jumped in—"come in and talk to you?"

"What about?"

"It's personal." Daf had recovered.

"No one can hear us. Really."

"Please?" Daf implored.

"Children, I'm very sorry, but—"

"Wait!" Daf broke in, positive the door was about to

slam on them. "See, I brought the thirty-five cents I owe you."

Rachel, puzzled, frowned . . . Of course!

"Well, with a clean dress, and an escort, you do look slightly different."

"Now can we come in?"

Rachel felt queer, apprehensive. Why this eagerness to come in? It couldn't be just to repay the token. The girl was making no motion to hand it over.

"I'm sorry"—she ventured what she hoped was a motherly smile—"some other time, when perhaps—"

"Let us tell you who we are," Daf blurted.

Rachel waited.

Daphne's mouth turned dry, stiff, unmovable.

"She's Daphne Beckman," Vick haltingly, reluctantly, came to her rescue, "and I'm her brother, Vick."

"And we can't stay too long anyhow," Daf, half-pleading, managed now to add.

Rachel, for a second, thought her knees might give. She breathed in deeply. Yup, Henry's kids all right. Better-looking than their pictures too. But what the hell were they . . . ? He stomach tightened, ached. She knew why they were here. Why else?

"You still want us to go away?" Daf asked, a little more confidently.

Rachel stepped back, motioned them to enter.

At the archway to the living room, Daphne stopped, struck by the room's curtains, great flowing pleats of lush gold silk framing the windows, with lustrous sheer see-throughs hung softly over the glass, and plush tassles, swags, huge gleaming brass knobs for the tiebacks.

"Come on in."

Then Vick cleared his throat.

Daphne blinked and edged in. Next to Vick there wasn't any seat. Nearby him on the floor? Or slide over one of those small French chairs?

"You got"—Vick broke the ice—"a very nice, gorgeous apartment."

"Thank you."

"And nice drapes too," Daf joined in.

Vick felt relieved. Daf polite. Maybe she'd even stay that way.

"Daphne, I like your dress."

"Thank you."

Daphne didn't want to sit near *her*. Maybe the best thing would be not to sit anywhere. *She* was pointing, though, to the cushion right next to hers. Daf, backing as casually as she could to the far end of the couch, awkwardly lowered herself.

"Well, tell me, does your dad know you people are here?"

"Oh, no."

"And you mustn't tell him, you mustn't," Daf implored.

"Then, uh, why, uh, I mean, what did he tell you about me?"

Daf shot a look at her brother. Coming here was *his* idea, so he ought to answer. He probably wouldn't, though.

"Madam, probably it's ridiculous, like really stupid, but . . ."

"Yes?"

Vick *was* brave! Daf's heart soared.

"See, the thing is," he continued, "it's about our father going away . . . with you."

"So, uh . . . *is* he?"

Rachel swallowed her gasp. These kids' words, hell, she'd expected. But not this child's glittering eyes, nor that desperate small voice. Tightening her robe about her, she stared back at Daphne, searching, something missing, what? Then, almost as if at a movie, pictures played across Rachel's mind, superimposing themselves over this anxious, thin face in the corner of her couch. First, Daphne running across the broad crosstown street toward her at the bus stop. Then the girl timorously stepping up to her, begging for thirty cents. On the bus, Daphne asking, "Write down your address?" Then pong, pong, pong, that noise out on the fire escape, Henry thrusting legs into pants, racing out the door, Daphne's frozen face loomed at her, immense. *Her!* God, that noise was her . . .

Daf knew why this woman wasn't answering, why she was making them wait and wait. Because she was thinking how to make up a perfect alibi. So she could lie.

"And don't you try and get out of it. 'Cause I saw you naked!"

"Shut up!" Vick yelled.

Rachel shuddered.

"Look, see"—Vick strained to soften, soothe, apologize— "I was supposed to do the talking."

Rachel nodded dully.

"So . . . *is* he"—Vick still had to have the answer— "going away?"

Rachel's shock gave way to awe, admiration even. This

child out on that fire escape. And now, coming all the way here.

"You kids have a lot of guts."

"Naw," Vick shrugged.

Daphne's eyes, smoldering still, stayed fixed on Rachel. "So are you going to take him away?"

Rachel sensed the terror beneath the anger.

"No."

"You're not?" Vick hardly dared believe he'd heard right.

"How could I? No one could take him away from you. You're his children. He loves you. But as far as where I fit in, that's a little complicated, and I think *he's* the one who should explain it."

"He already has!" Daf itched to spit back. Bursting, she had to get up, move, do something. At a console table against the wall, she picked up a delicate-looking china figurine, fondled it. You could break it so easy too.

"What if I gave you all my government bonds? One every birthday. From the bank. Then you can go to Portofino. Like Harriet on *Secret of Life*. That's where she met this great piano player, and she forgot all about her old boy friend."

Rachel felt both like laughing and crying.

"Well?"

"That's a generous offer, Daphne."

"I mean it. You can have those bonds. Every single one."

Rachel rose. "How about a cold drink?"

"Really, I promise. And that's a lot of money."

"I know. Fruit juice? Coke? Milk?"

Mrs. Nyland had left. Daf let her head plop back against the couch cushion. She'd known always, all along. She wished they'd never come here.

Rachel couldn't seem to keep a grasp on the Coke bottle. Even after she dried it with a paper towel, it slipped, tipped and almost fell. Finally she locked it still against a sponge, but then the cap wouldn't budge. Her forearm felt as if it weren't hers. It belonged on some other body. A limb made of styrofoam. No strength at all.

Children? What did you bring me, what did you bring me, ice-cream-smeared faces, kitchens decorated with their screamingly wild free drawings—but what did she really know about them? And Henry, for all his marvelous funny stories about them—did he know them? She tried to remember herself as a girl, letting loose an avalanche of passion. Yes, she could recall hitting her mother, something about a doll. Had it been taken away from her? And if you compared a father to a doll, well . . .

With every ounce of her strength, Rachel squeezed the bottle and yanked the opener, and the cap bent up, carbon dioxide whooshing out.

She did like them, she decided. And after a few more horrors like today, probably they could start liking her too.

Glasses lightly clinking against each other, or ice cubes, slipper trods. Daf opened her eyes. Mrs. Nyland returning with drinks on a tray.

"Could I use your bathroom?"

"Sure." Rachel pointed.

Daf hurried out.

Instead of going into the open bathroom, she peeked back over her shoulder, and then cut into the doorway alongside. Geez, a round bed. How would you keep from falling off it? She poked through the chiffony curtains. The window had an air conditioner, and it was sealed too. She tried the other window. The drop down to the courtyard was sheer.

Back out in the hallway she hesitated. No, the little bathroom window would be dumb. 'Cause if there was a fire, how could a grown person ever fit himself through it?

Sun streamed in the kitchen window, and, yes, right outside were black up-and-down bars that had to be for a fire-escape railing. Hurrying to it, she stopped short. Was this a gas stove? The color of metal-steel, and so shiny . . . maybe it wasn't. She turned a knob. Fire, a ring of blue flame. So it did *too* have to be gas! The window, she saw, had a lock on it, but only the easy screw kind. So try it. But what if Mrs. fancy bathrobe decided she was missing awful long, and came looking?

Daf glided speedily back to the door. Vick's and her voice sounded talking back and forth nice and easy. She scooted back to the window, pushed a chair next to it, clambered up, and tried to turn, unloosen the screw lock. She struggled, wrenched hard. It gave, and then it began to unscrew, easily.

CHAPTER 11

"D-a-a-phne-e-e!" A voice bellowed, echoed, shattering the prim street's Sunday-morning stillness. "Hey! Hey, Daf!" It grew louder even, closer.

Sonny-James? Yup, she turned and saw him, arms outstretched, making a V in the air, loping toward them with big strides.

"Hi. G'mornin'. Where you been hidin'? This here your boy frien'? He's a pretty good-lookin' fella."

She didn't want to talk. What for? Best thing would be to keep going, make believe she hadn't heard, like he wasn't even there. Except he was standing right in her path, tree-trunk legs, going up ten miles high.

Vick, off a bit to the side, broke the strained silence. "I'm her brother. I'm Vick."

"How you be, Vick? Sonny-James Parker here, pleased to know ya."

She waited while Vick, a little dazedly, got his miniature hand shook by Sonny-James' huge one. Then she began to edge around and move past him.

"Hey, where you rushin' to? You mad at me or somethin'?"

"No. Not really."

"Well, then?"

"I guess it's just, we're very busy."

The bushy beard rose and fell slowly, nodding, and the hairy man throatily murmured, "Ohhhh," like he understood every thought in her head, and felt sorry about them too.

"So"—Daf felt a twinge of guilt now—"so long."

She reached for Vick and tugged at his arm. He, eyes wide as saucers, as if staring at a ghost or fairy creature, seemed rooted to the sidewalk.

"Say, that trouble you was tellin' me about, gettin' all your toys stole, yeah, and your house burned down, that ain't the kind of busy you're into now, is it?"

"What do you care?"

"I thought we was friends."

"You did?"

Solemnly he nodded, "Sure did."

"Yeah, but friends help each other." Her flicker of hope had quickly soured. "And you wouldn't."

"How 'bout an ice cream?"

"No, thank you."

"Excuse us, mister," Vick chimed in, coolly, his eyes shrunk back to normal, "but we have to go home now."

"Okay, whyn't I take you?" Sonny-James pointed to an open-top flamingo-colored sports car, exotic, almost supersonic-looking, parked across the street.

Vick's jaw sagged. "In that?"

"Un hunh."

The first part of the way, Sonny-James sang. A sad song about waiting for his sweet woman to come home, nothing on his mind but waiting for her to come on home. Then, as they entered the park, he excitedly started pointing out stuff: trees, people riding horses, kids with balloons, baseball bats, girls in hot pants. "Look, ain't that somethin'? Now what about that? See, who says it's so bad? Never is, long as you keep on tryin'. Take my woman. Won' see me, won' see me, no she will not see me. Then one mornin', today, I give her a call up from the lobby, you know, on the house phone, and after like a thousand tries, she says, fine, let's have lunch. You see!"

Daphne, jammed in next to him, kept getting jabbed and poked as he shifted, braked, steered. Swinging quickly between lanes, his elbow gave her a particularly painful dig. She bit her lip to keep from crying out. Weird, he hadn't noticed. All those bones, muscles, bulging into her, and he didn't feel a thing. His fingers gripped the wheel like it was a puny piece of wire. His wrist looked a million times as thick. Yup, he might be almost as strong as Private Eye. Stronger even? And maybe—maybe she'd been wrong about him—being like every other grownup. 'Cause look how he was today, driving them, singing. And even if he hadn't ever got rid of anybody, he sure knew how. 'Cause he must have seen a lot more TV and movies, 'cause he was so old.

But could you be sure about him? He didn't seem sneaky like a stool pigeon, unless he might be . . . a preacher in disguise. God could have sent him to ambush them, or the F.B.I. Boy, how could you really, really find out? Still, if he promised not to tell, and stuck to it, then God maybe had to be on their side. Specially if he agreed to help and be captain.

"Sonny?"

He hadn't heard. It was awful windy-noisy, with no

roof over them. She felt his leg move. A red light ahead, braking, muscles hardening, pressing into her. They stopped. Now, ask him now. But—but how could you? In a second they'd be moving in the traffic again. And then they were. She could ask maybe for his number, and phone him. Yeah, that way she could talk it over with Vick first. No, he'd say no. Vick's eyes were fixed straight ahead, and she could tell he didn't even like getting this free ride.

"No, no, further down"—Vick was pointing—"toward the end of the block."

The car was creeping now, quietly, and you *could* talk, but there wasn't any time left. In a second, they'd have to get out.

"No, the next house, the one right after this."

Vick, she saw, was already squeezing down the door handle.

"Good-bye. Thank you. C'mon, Daf."

She didn't want to go up. There had to be plenty of time still till lunch. Maybe . . . he'd take her to a playground again.

"You kids hungry?"

She wasn't really, but . . .

"How 'bout an ice cream now?"

"No, thank you." Vick, up on the sidewalk, was already partway toward the door.

She hadn't moved.

"You coming?"

"Vick."

"Yeah?"

"Tell Mom, well, tell her . . ."

"What?"

"Oh, I don't know. That I made friends with someone. I'll be back, I'll be right back in a little while."

He shrugged and went in.

Double parked outside the Carvel store on Broadway, Daf was licking the chocolate topping off her cone. The custard underneath started to melt and drip onto her fingers, so she began taking bites. Quickly she got the cream down level with the top of the cone, so she could talk.

"You think the cops could ever trace a glass cutter?"

"How—how do you mean?"

"You know, the way they trace guns."

He scratched his head, "Don' know for sure, but I wouldn't espect so."

"Why not?"

"We-e-ell, your glass cutter won' have a serial number, now will it?"

Yeah, that's right. She felt a surge of gladness and relief. And geez, he was smart too. Not just strong.

He told her he had a whole hour before he had to go have lunch, and asked if she might like to go for a ride with him.

"Okay, sure."

He veered down a ramp off the West Side Highway, and drove through what had to be the narrowest streets, with the tallest buildings anywhere. And almost no people or cars. They stopped. Here suddenly there was space and light. The building they'd parked in front of, a straight-up black skyscraper, was set way way back from the street, with a broad patio of pink slabs leading to it. And something really wild too, a bright red cube, tremendous, high, two stories maybe, but balanced somehow so it stood on one of its corners, diamond-shaped sort of.

"That's a Noguchi sculpture."

Nearing it, Daf saw, cut right through it, a big round hole. You could see the sky up through it. What was it doing? Could it really be just for fun?

He led her on between the black tower and an old building with cement wreaths and imitation columns molded onto its walls, across a little street, and then to an even larger open space, ringed by more skyscrapers and one especially huge one. At its foot a double row of new-looking trees lined one side of the plaza, in whose center a railing went around to make a wide circle.

"That there's a sculpture garden."

Daf leaned against the railing and looked down—the garden was way below—but it was just big stones, arranged like in the museum. Around its perimeter was all glass, big windows, stores maybe.

"Like it?"

"Why'd you bring me here?"

"'Cause it's beautiful. Makes me feel how great people can be, what fine stuff they can do when they get the chance."

What's so great about some stones? She didn't say that, though.

"I'm disappointed."

"You are?"

"I thought you'd dig this place."

"Oh, I do. It's . . . fantastic. Only I have to get home. And . . . I have to talk to you."

Strolling back to the car, Daf leaned her head back, counting how many floors. At seventeen, she blinked, and had to start over. On the second blink, she gave up. So many windows, millions, and in every one, somebody's daddy worked. Were they all going away too?

"Well?"

"Hunh?"

"Thought you said you *had* to talk to me."

"Oh. Yes. Well, uh, do you believe in secrets?"

"Sure. Sometimes."

"What about promises?"

"What about them?"

"Did you ever break one?"

"No. Don't think so. Why?"

"You know."

"You gonna just have to trust me, or not tell me."

They'd reached the car. Daf wanted to climb in and shut the door, and to keep walking. To stay with him, and run back over to the giant cube. To be home at the TV with Vick, and to tell Sonny-James.

"Hey, no sweat, Daf. Maybe some other time you'll be more in the mood."

He swung the car door open for her.

"But"—she wasn't moving—"I might never see you again."

"Not if we keep bumpin' into each other, the way we been doin'."

She noticed the dashboard light was on. Sure, because of the open door, and he still was holding it for her. The worst thing would be, she'd get sent to reform school. Well, so what. That'd teach Daddy. Serve him right.

"You gettin' in?"

"Now don't forget, you promised."

"Oh, you're gonna tell me, hunh."

"Promise?"

"You got a deal."

Swinging her head around, she swept the street with her eyes. They were alone. Sunday no one came here.

"Feel like sittin'? And we can talk while I drive you back?"

"That's too noisy."

"Oh."

"See—see, there's this woman. And we asked her not to, and she wouldn't listen, and neither will my father. So we've got to stop her."

"Uh, what did you ask this woman?"

"Oh. Well, not to take him away."

"Him?"

"My father!"

"Oh. Yeah, I see what you mean."

"You do? Oh, I knew you would."

"So how you figure on doin' that? Stoppin' her, I mean?"

"That's the hard part. I think we're going to have to sneak in through the fire escape. Only I'm not sure we can do it. 'Cause my brother might chicken out, or change his mind. So I might need help."

"Okay, so you sneak in there. How's that gonna stop her?"

"Oh, yeah, I forgot. We turn on the gas stove."

"Yeah"—he nodded slowly—"yeah, I guess I can see where you *might* need a little extra help."

"See, this way my daddy'll stay home, and maybe move us back to Cedarhurst, and then I wouldn't have to bother you any more."

"You gonna write books someday, Daphne? That's the kinda haid you got."

"So you give me your phone number, and then I'll call you when we have to get things really ready."

"Okay, sure, you call me."

He took out his wallet, pulled a card from it, wrote down some figures, and handed her the slip of cardboard.

"You going to stay around New York, or are you going back out West?"

"Oh, I'll be aroun'. Long enough."

"Yeah?"

"Come on. Let's get you home."

Grinning, she climbed in.

"Say"—he smiled back, enjoying her contentment—"this lady, I mean, you goin' to tell me somethin' more about her?"

"Like what?"

"Oh, her name, where she lives, that kind of stuff."

"That's a secret."

"Oh, okay."

He started the car.

"But I'll tell you."

"You don't have to."

"Her name's Mrs. Nyland. And she's really not so bad-looking. It's in that house, you know, where you were putting up the cockamamies."

Beneath the thick beard, Daphne couldn't see the color drain from his skin.

CHAPTER 12

Hugging close to the store windows and doorways was slowing her down. Daf wanted to hurry, move out into the middle of the sidewalk, get it over with; but when someone passed, she'd stop, turn in, and pretend to be looking at Panasonic TVs, or wedding and first-communion photos, or a Miss Rheingold display. It had started off seeming so smart, going three blocks down Amsterdam, instead of to the hardware store around the corner on Broadway. But now she was worried. People weren't only looking at her, they were turning and looking. So what? Maybe she did look funny. She sort of had to. Still, they'd never recognize her. And if a policeman stopped her, or anybody, she could say she was going to a costume party, even if it wasn't Halloween.

But she still felt mad. She'd thought and thought, figuring how to get disguised. And then putting it all on in front of the mirror had been so groovy, and made her feel safe, invisible even. It wasn't fair it should turn out just the opposite. A woman pushing a shopping cart in one direction was staring back at Daf in the other. Did she look that freaky? In front of a store that had no awning, "Discos Latinos," she paused, rechecked her reflection: floppy broad-brimmed hat, Mom's ash-blond casual tousled wig, sun glasses, Mom's old paisley brocade jacket with its collar turned up, her pink pedal pushers, which on Daf looked almost like bell bottoms, light-blue rubber gloves. Yeah, it was queer. She still could stop, go back, try putting on some different stuff. She looked up at the street sign. But only one more block to that store. Clenching, digging fingernails into her palms, she pushed ahead.

Solowey's Hardware & Locksmith. She peered through the plate glass. Glass cutters, where were they? Would they be displayed in the window—so maybe even before she went in, she could pick out which one she wanted? Locks, brassy, a whole row lined up down front: "Mortise Type Colonial Design, $23.99; Exterior Lock, 5-Pin Tumbler, ONLY $6.89!; Beautiful HEAVY-DUTY PROTECTION with 6-Pin Tumbler and Extra Long 1/2-Inch Bolt Throw, ONLY $11.79!; Secure NIGHT LOCK, 8-Pin Cylinder, Double-Fitted Key Can Be Duplicated Only At Factory, JIMMY-PROOF, $19.75." Behind, up on a platform, were three wood-grained boxes, like small hi-fi speakers, backed by a large sign in bold blue lettering: "NEW ULTRASONIC INTRUDER ALARM, LATEST TECHNOLOGY, Inaudible Soundwaves Detect Movement and Sound The Alarm, Used In Banks, Warehouses And Military Installations, $109.50. Easy-As-Pie Installation. FREE DEMONSTRATION." Wearily, Daf leaned her forehead against the glass. How could you beat that, unless you came from outer space? And had special ears?

Racking her brain, motionless for a minute or an hour, Daf thought. Program after program whirred through her head. Finally, yes, before Private Eye caught him, that hunchback, he got into the museum, and no alarms ever went off. 'Cause first the basement, the fuse, sure, first he unscrewed the fuse. Besides, Sonny-James would know even more ways to stop those things.

She pulled the heavy door open and went in. Up behind the cash register, her eye was caught by an array of gleaming tools: hammers, screwdrivers, drills, chisels. No people, they all seemed to be off in the back. Swinging around, she looked up at the opposite wall, shelves lined with cans: "Monsanto Mothballs, Kane's Guaranteed Cockroach Killer, Miller's Rat Poison, XXX, Keep Away From Children."

"Yes?"

Daf started, then turned. A lady, her face crisscrossed with wrinkles, older-looking than Grandma Edna even, short, hardly taller than Daf herself, was shuffling toward her.

"Sveetheart, can I 'elp you?"

Daf, just as she'd practiced, held out her arm. The slip of paper, with everything written down so it was supposed to look like a note from Mom, fluttered between her fingers. The old lady, though, didn't take it. She was staring at Daf.

"You going to a party, hunh."

Daf nodded.

"You going to vin de prize."

Daf, smiling a thank you, nodded again, more vigorously, and waved her list.

The lady finally reached for it, crinkled her brow as she read down it, and then looked queerly at Daf.

Daf shrugged, innocently, as if to say, "That's what

my mother wants. Can I help it?", then dropped her eyes to the floor, and waited.

The old lady hobbled off toward the back, muttering indistinctly.

Daf stood in a corner, so maybe no one else would notice her. Inches from her nose were decorated teakettles, Teflon-coated griddles, stainless-steel mixing bowls. The shelves piled with utensils and pots, porcelainized in orange, green, yellow, blue, and no porcelain, just plain silvery color—endless. Ting, bing-bong, the cash register rang. Change clinked on the counter. "Thank you. Come again. So long now. Bye." How much longer? Her legs began to ache. What if you had to be eighteen, like for when Daddy sent her for Jack Daniel bourbon whiskey, and the man wouldn't sell it? Or if the lady said the price was more than twenty dollars and twelve cents, 'cause that's all there was in the pocketbook. Daf shot a sideways glance toward the door. She could make a break for it maybe, if she had to.

Halting, clopping footsteps coming closer, on top of her almost, and then sounds of metal, plastic, crinkly paper, hitting against each other and the counter top.

"Okay, honey. Okay."

Daf turned. The old lady, she saw, was panting slightly.

"Okay, you ready?"

Daf nodded. But what was she supposed to be ready for?

"Pencil flash wit two extra batteries," she read from the list, then pointed to the thin pocket light, "polyetylene tape, greaseless lubricant—Dis ɪᴛ is da cat's meow. You tell your momma I recomment—carbide glass cutter—

mine last one, I gotta reorder—eight feet shower tubing. Saran Wrap you get in de supermarket. Wit a glass cutter your daddy don't need maybe glazing putty?"

Daphne shook her head.

"Clamps, for dis tubing? Old rusty clamps iss no good, you know."

Again Daf shook, forcing herself to smile too.

"Okay, dear." The lady pushed spectacles up her nose against her eyes, poised a finger over the register, but then turned back to Daphne. "How come you wearing rubber gloves?"

Suddenly Daf couldn't breathe, her nostrils clogged, or was it her chest? Run? Leave everything when it was right here in front of her? No. She took a deep breath, reached across the counter for a pencil, and wrote on the pad alongside, "I have leprosy and impetigo."

The old lady took an abrupt step back. Her glasses slipped back down her frozen nose.

Kneeling on the kitchen-floor linoleum, in front of the stove, Daphne tore a strip of tape from the broad spool, and was extra careful to keep it from sticking to her clothes or the floor. She had a sudden urge to stop, stretch out on her back and rest; but the timer up on the counter had already started clicking away again, and this time, her third try, she had to prove to Vick it wasn't baloney, that she really could do the whole thing in three minutes—and with rubber gloves on too.

Completing a cross with the hole in the middle, she attached the last of the four strips of polyethylene across the open oven, two vertical now and two horizontal, and then fitted the funnel through the center hole—narrow end facing out. Next she rolled out some Saran, and covered the whole oven opening with the clear plastic film, fixing it in place with more tape, except for the bottom, through which she reached up and poked a hole in the plastic with the thin end of the funnel. Reaching behind her for the rubber tubing, she looked at her brother, crosslegged against the refrigerator. Their eyes met. He was still watching, he hadn't turned off. She felt glad, but just for a second. He didn't look too thrilled.

Getting the tubing onto the funnel was the hardest. Before, both times, the funnel had slipped away and fallen back into the oven without getting connected. This time she gripped its neck between her fingers, tightly but not too hard, or she'd tear the Saran, while she prodded and pressed, struggling to get the rubber around and on top of the aluminum. RRRRrrrng! The timer again, damn! She didn't look up, though, just kept working, inching the rubber further and further around the metal. Would an inch be firm enough? She pulled gently. It held, it was!

"See." She felt proud.

Vick, mouth open, shook his head, awed—but not too happy.

"Only," Daf sighed, "I got to keep practicing. So I can do it faster."

"What about that?" He pointed to the door, where Daf had tilted a vinyl-covered, chrome-legged kitchen chair in under the knob, so she'd have a minute to stash everything in the oven if Mom suddenly came in.

She looked up at the clock. Five to four. Mom might pop in any second for her cold coffee. Yeah, better quit. Quickly, but carefully so as not to leave little snippets stuck around, she ripped off the tape and Saran, stuffed it into a brown paper grocery bag, put the funnel back into the bottom cupboard where it belonged, stuck the rubber tubing into her schoolbag, and hurried off to throw the brown bag down the incinerator.

Vick was staring out the window when she came back.

"You know," he said, not turning or looking at her, "she must be rich."

"What's so rich about her?"

"*We* don't have any doorman, do we?"

"You think that's why—all of this—'cause she's rich?"

"What if all we did was rob her, take everything away, so she gets poor?"

"You'd have to get movers. Besides, being rich is mostly all in banks."

A long silent minute passed, broken abruptly by his turning and taking a few fast steps to the corner of the counter, where Mom's junk mail, magazines, all kinds of papers were piled. He lifted the phone off the heap and began shuffling through grocery lists, Estée Lauder skin-cream circulars, *New York Review of Books*, *West Side Pennysavers*, a Burpee seed catalogue.

"Whatcha looking for?"

Not answering, his fingers steadily turning up the tops of pages, he leafed through "*I. F. Stone's Weekly*"; "BIG SAVINGS with WISK coupons"; "Books!—Reductions Up To 83%." Then he stopped. He was reading, and not just the first line. He pulled from the pile a narrow brochure, its cover adorned with half a man's face, split down the center from hair to chin.

"What's that? What did you find?"

"The New Theater at Saint Paul's. An attempt at rad-i-cal," Vick read, beginning to stumble on the long words, "re-struc-turing to bring into being the theater of today."

"Hunh? What's that for?"

"Two thirty-six Ninth Avenue."

"So?"

"That's the address."

She shrugged, opened the refrigerator, took out a carton of milk, and poured into her blue plastic glass.

"It's where Daddy is now, where they're rehearsing." He laid the glossy paper-fold on the table in front of her.

A quick glance at it back and front, she pushed it away, and said, "That's just a crummy old church."

"So what if it is."

"So someday I'm going to buy him a real theater. Radio City."

"We ought to go over there and talk to him."

Her head hurt, and her tummy, and her chest. He was going to double-cross her. She felt like punching-slapping-clawing him. "Liar!" she hissed, trembling. "You said the only place we had to go was her house."

Vick tried to remember. He'd never said, the *only* place, had he? But it'd be crazy to argue. Not while she was so exploding.

How could she hit him? Then he'd get mad too, and he'd never ever help. She plunked herself down on the floor, crawled under the table, and shut her eyes.

Vick drank some milk, and waited for her to come out. Getting itchy, finally he crouched down and joined her. Her nose, he saw, was dribbling. He went back out, and got her some paper towels.

"Thanks."

"You gone crazy?"

"I promised Daddy I'd never tell."

"So—so I'll tell him you never told me."

"He'll think I'm a liar."

Vick stuck the fleshy part of his forefinger into his mouth and chewed on it, thinking. "Look, what if you had a nightmare? You were talking in your sleep, and I heard you."

"You don't sleep in my room."

"Yeah, but what if you had a bellyache, and you didn't want to be alone, and *then* you had a nightmare."

"He'll never believe that."

Vick reached up and dug with his fingernail at an encrustation, some old food probably, on the bottom edge of the table. After a while, still scraping at it, he asked, "Did you beg him?"

Daf began to crawl out. Any second, she knew, they'd be in a fight. She had to stop, though. He was holding her ankle.

"Did you really beg for him not to go?"

"No . . . I mean, I wanted to . . . Only I couldn't."

Vick let go of her foot.

"We're not going out anywhere with that stuff"—he pointed to the briefcase with the tubing—"till I—beg him."

"When?"

"Now."

Daf crawled out, put the carton of milk back into the refrigerator, and said, "You're the one who's crazy."

"You coming?"

"You'll see. And you'll be sorry."

CHAPTER 13

Up at the corner, half a block away still, that had to be it. Daf knew because of the huge round window, in color, slanted roof, thick solid look of the place—unless once they got to the cross street, there'd be another church, across the avenue maybe. Or three churches, and Daddy wouldn't be in any of them. That'd show Vick, once and for all maybe.

Coming abreast of the church's back wall, they began passing a high black wrought-iron fence which ran along its side. Between the metal and the mauve-maroon stone wall, there were plants—weeds, a long narrow patch rising from between cobblestones. This fence, what if it continued all the way around, a complete circle, so there'd be no way ever to get in? So Daddy couldn't be in there either. Besides, why would he want to be? Who would ever come to see a show here, where it was so grimy-dirty-looking, if they could go to Radio City?

At the corner, though, the fence ended, and the church entrance did front the street. She looked around for a marquee, a ticket-seller's booth, anything to tell you where the theater part was. She saw only broad steps, an enormous door, not even any windows. Across the street and next door were just old tenements, one after the other. Checking them sure didn't seem worth it.

"Hey, c'mere!"

Vick was pointing to a glass-enclosed sign built into the stone.

Daf rushed to join him. "St. Paul's Methodist Church, Reverend Oliver Beigbeder . . ." Her eyes raced over the white replaceable letters set into a grooved black backing, and then quickly dropped to the bottom, which read, "A New Play, SO WHO SAYS I'M A FAILURE?, by Henry Beckman, will open Thurs. June 11 and run through June 28. Reservations at the Vestry 2–5."

So this *was* where. But still, maybe now Daddy wouldn't be here. Instead, maybe they'd meet a kindly old priest, who'd invite them to stay for dinner, with a roaring fireplace, and then take them off to the country, a lake, for a canoe trip, and way out in the middle of the water, that's where they'd meet God.

Vick, at the head of the broad steps, gripped the large knob with both hands, managed to turn it, pulled. The door would not give, not even a sliver of an inch. He tried pushing. It wouldn't budge that way either. He knocked hard. That hurt his knuckles, though. And the sound wasn't even loud. The bottom of the door had a brass plate. He tried kicking it. Still no answer. Ruefully he looked back at his sister on the sidewalk. The smirk on her face said, "I told you so." She was wrong. Daddy *had* to be in there. He put his ear to the massive portal. Yes, sounds, music, voices. Nothing clear, but people were in there.

Could there be another door?

A walkway along the other side, and then, yes! And it pulled out, light as a feather. Vick began the plunge in, turned, and saw Daf standing a distance back, making no move to follow.

"Come on."

"You go. I'll wait for you."

He went and took her hand. Stiffly, robotlike, but not really resisting, she let herself be led.

A last beam of brightness going in, and darkness swallowed them. Still, huddled against one another, they waited. Soon maybe their eyes would adjust, they'd be able to see. Yes, more doors ahead, the place was tiny, a vestibule. Again Vick pulled Daf forward with him.

More darkness, except hard to the right, in the sanctuary, was a brilliantly lit platform, a stage sort of, with people moving, yelling, singing on it. Except it had no curtain or frame, like in the school auditorium. Ahead Vick now could see pews, rows and rows disappearing off into the gloom. Was Daddy back in there?

"Nah, nah, nah, nah!" Shrieks from the stage made him turn. Upside down in a yoga position, naked except for shorts, Vick saw a man, fat bulging belly, kicking his short legs, and moaning now. Circling him, holding a hypodermic big as a bicycle pump, coming closer and closer, making feints and jabs through the air at him with it, was a nurse, wearing clown makeup—solid red nose, huge lips. Then hovering over him, her arm poised way back, ready, suddenly plunging down . . .

Daf snapped shut her eyes, shuddering.

"Cut, cut! Peter, what in Christ happened this time?" an angry high-pitched voice shouted from the rear.

"It's not my fault!" a man with an even higher voice shouted back.

Daf opened her eyes again and discovered that the actors on the platform had gone.

"Peter, would you shake your ass"—the first voice was cooler now—"and for once in your life get that frigging music cue right!"

"Gabe, I *told* you this Japanese piece of shit would slip. Well, the darling slipped. Now I'll give you your mother-loving music on cue, but I need a decent tape recorder."

Daf smiled, and saw Vick was grinning too. She nudged him. It was funny hearing cursing from grownups like that. Now this place seemed not quite so scary. They both still had their backs pressed against the door, though, ready to flee, just in case.

"Hi."

A young man with a beard suddenly was standing right next to them.

Daf, startled, pushed against the door with all her might. Not fast enough, though. Her arm, it was being gripped—gently.

"You kids can stay. Everything we do here is wide open to the community. But come on in the back, and then take a seat. You'll see better. And the actors aren't too comfortable when you're so close."

The kids followed him into the gloom. Halting, he motioned them into a pew.

Vick began sidestepping in, then stopped short. "We're looking for Mr. Beckman."

"Who?"

"The author."

"He means," Daf added, "like the writer."

"Oh, sure, Hank. He's here. I'll get him."

"Top of seven, let's go already!" the commanding, high-pitched voice shouted.

Daf and Vick sat.

A moment later total darkness again, along with the sounds of bombs exploding, or buildings being demolished, or volcanos, which modulated somehow to violins, but snarling like angry bees. At the same time, bursts of colored light flared about the stage, with the over-all illumination growing brighter and brighter. Now they could make out the roly-poly man from before, still in his shorts, but this time sitting cross-legged on a tall pedestal. Costumed characters, each pinioned to a small cross —Mickey Mouse was the only one Daf recognized—began parading across the stage. Suddenly the man in underwear leaped down. Daf was surprised he didn't seem to have hurt himself. Stepping as close to the audience edge of the platform as he could, he said, "Which one first? How do I decide?" The people with the crosses on their backs and arms laughed mockingly, stuck out their tongues at him, and began speaking, hissing, shouting, "Decide? Decide? Decide? You? you? YOU?, their voices and laughter becoming amplified, electronically distorted, grotesque—making Daphne's ears hurt.

Her shoulder too? No, something tapping it, softly, then a finger brushing over the back of her neck. She'd scream. Who would hear her, though, in all this noise?

She turned, saw a hand, looked up—Daddy! In the row behind, bent over toward her, he was beckoning for her to come out to the aisle.

"Vick!"

He didn't seem to hear.

She nudged him.

Caught up in the wildness on stage, he didn't seem to feel that either.

She poked two fingers hard into his side.

Out in the close, dark vestibule, Henry, hugging them, kept trying to imagine why they were here. A message from Joanne? No, more likely they'd come without her permission, and he'd have to end up laying down the law, a little anyway. But regardless, their trekking all the way down here to see him, be with him—nice.

"What's up?"

Daf waited for her brother to explain. Only he didn't. "This was Vick's idea."

"Oh?"

"Dad, uh, do people in church theaters talk like that all the time?"

Henry chuckled. He should send them on their way, he knew, and get back inside. That faggot director had to be watched every second. In an hour he could change half the lines, turn the play into something unrecognizable. And yet, he felt glad to be out, that the kids had given him this excuse to slip away, to stop worrying about every actor's every gesture, word, movement, the missed music cues.

"You have," Daf asked, "to stay here much longer?"

"Probably, yes."

"And you can't"—Vick was half pleading—"leave for a little while?"

"Why?"

Vick ached to get on with it, tell him, beg him. But these doors on both sides, ten million people could walk right in. And it was too dark.

"Is something wrong? Did something happen to your mother? You two are all right, aren't you?"

"Oh sure, fine," Vick answered quickly. That at least was easy to say.

The door from within pushed open partway.

"Henry?"

"Yes?"

"They're taking a break. And what are you doing? Why did you come out here?"

Daf wanted to die. *Her*. Her voice. She'd recognized it instantly. Only it was too late to run.

Light, the outside door, painful brightness poured in. Vick was leaning against it, pushing it open.

Rachel was first to recover enough to speak.

"Well, hello."

Henry, in his imagination, had sweated through this scene, introducing Ray to the kids, a thousand times. They'd all meet—at the zoo, an outdoor restaurant, her apartment. It'd be stiff, then violent—explosive sometimes. Weird, how it had sneaked up on him here in this cramped, dim church doorway.

They began the hand-shaking ceremony, awkwardly, when doors swung open, and actors and technicians started streaming through. "Hi, Hank. Can I get you a sandwich? . . . Oh hi, Hank, want to join us for an ice cream? . . . Hank, what are you doing here in the dark? You still gotta come and try that pizzeria down the block." Softly, but with unmistakable firmness, he spoke his sorries and no thank yous, cutting off possible questions about the children and what they might be doing here. To decide was the problem. He felt so torn. Was right now the time to tell the kids who Ray really was? And her, would she mind, feel hurt, if he waited? And what about—would Daphne recognize her?

Rachel, when the initial shock abated, sensed that Henry didn't know. The kids obviously hadn't told about their visit to her. They *knew*, and he didn't know they knew. That put her and them, in a sense, in some kind of league together, which felt so wrong. She hadn't wanted to tell, to worry Henry, not while he so badly needed a clear head for the play. But should she tell him now?

Vick, seeing her, had felt a sharp pang in his stomach, and in his chest too. *She*, this woman, came to Daddy's rehearsals. Not him, or Daf, or Mom, but *she* did. Daf maybe *was* smarter.

Henry suggested a cold drink, and they all ambled, bunched together, along the brick pathway toward the street.

Daf caught at her brother's arm, then waited while Dad and *her* moved a few steps ahead. "Well?" she stated almost more than asked.

"What do you mean?"

"*She* comes to his rehearsal."

Did Daf think he was blind?

He didn't answer, though, because they were just catching up to the grownups on the sidewalk.

Rachel turned back to them. "Good-bye, kids."

"Where you going?" Henry was surprised.

"I think they probably want to be with their dad, exclusively. They sure didn't come all the way down here to see me. Right, kids?"

"You can stay," Vick replied almost too promptly, and then wondered why he'd said it. Now was he afraid to be alone with Dad?

"I do have some work of my own I've got to get done for tomorrow."

"Ray, stay. You'll enjoy them."

"I'm sure I would. But another time, I think." She spoke warmly, but with decision. He'd have to tell them, alone, in his own way, when *he* was ready—so that her role would be clear, firmly set. Then, and only then, would it make sense even to start trying to become their friend.

"Bye."

The Beckmans mumbled replies.

Vick raced after her, grabbed her hand, pulled her back to them—in his daydream.

The luncheonette had a big humming fan, but no air conditioner. Two flies buzzed above their little table in the back, alighting fleetingly on the greasy-looking lemon wall, diving at crumbs on the long narrow counter. Daddy, while waiting for the Puerto Rican counterman to bring their sodas, was explaining about the crosses, how not only Christ was killed when he didn't deserve to be, but lots of men and women, all through history, like Joan of Arc, some great ancient Greeks, Puritans . . .

Suddenly Daf jumped up, clapped her hands in midair, peeked into her palms, broke into a smile, and gleefully displayed the blackish speck.

Vick, grimacing, knew now the hard stuff had to begin. Daddy was looking down at the formica, as if he'd forgotten all about his story.

"You know, I still have no idea why it is you kids came down here."

"See"—Vick at least felt prepared—"the other night Daf didn't feel so good."

"Oh?"

"Yeah, that night after she stayed out late with you."

"How—what was wrong with you, Daf?"

Daf shrugged. This was all Vick's idea. Let him do it.

"You know, like she couldn't sleep. So she came into my room. Nightmares. And then she was talking in her sleep."

Henry thought of Rachel sailing off. So canny. She'd intuited so exactly why the kids had come, and recognized too that this was *his* thing. Christ, if only it weren't.

"Uh, don't you want to know"—Vick began to worry maybe Daddy wasn't ever going to ask—"what she said?"

"I can imagine."

Daf realized Daddy knew everything, that she hadn't kept her promise. She wanted to crawl under the table—vanish.

The counterman set down the sodas, sloppily, letting them drip over their sides, and not bothering to wipe up either.

Immediately Daf plunged in her straw and began sipping.

Now. Vick cleared his throat. Now. He couldn't wait more, or he'd never say it. "Daddy, we came, both of us, so we could beg you, like not to go away."

Henry had expected just this, more or less. But the words themselves, so naked, to the point, burned into him.

"I *told* him not to ask you!" Daf knew Daddy *had* to be furious, or he'd be answering. "I told him, but he wouldn't listen to me."

Henry reached across the table and took Daf's hand. She was suffering. She shouldn't be. "It's all right, Daf. It's fine for him to ask for anything, at any time. Both of you, you mustn't ever be afraid to ask me things. Okay?"

Daf stared down at the little foam bubbles, bursting one by one and drowning in her soda.

Henry got up and crouched by her chair. "You didn't say okay."

"Daddy, people are looking."

"So what?"

"Okay. So I said okay."

He kissed her quickly and slipped back to his seat.

Vick's fingers locked about the sugar container. Daddy still hadn't told about his going away, or not going. Probably he was, and Daf was right again. Except what if maybe it had been a nightmare?

"Dad?"

"Yes, son."

"That stuff you told Daf, well, is that for real?"

"Yes."

"We'll be perfect behaviors," Daf blurted. "We'll do the dishes every night, and take the wash down to the basement, and help shop the groceries, and Mom'll never get mad any more, we'll help so much."

"Look, if you really want us to ask you stuff, well"—Vick was pleading—"hasn't there got to be something so we can make you change your mind?"

Henry felt faint—the heat. He'd let them hypnotize him. He'd forget Ray. God, two such glorious children.

"Kids, nothing bad is going to happen to you. You must believe me." . . . Answer? Please? Just nod, at least . . . No, why should they? . . . "Look, I might sleep a few blocks away. But even now, we don't see each other when we're sleeping, do we?"

Vick began spooning the ice cream out of his glass before it all melted.

She didn't care any more if Daddy stayed or left, Daf decided. Only that woman—she'd never have him either.

CHAPTER 14

Vick hovered a hand above the on-off knob, while the Yanks trotted in toward their dugout, second half of the fourth. Should he shut off the dumb TV, or not? He should be loving every minute, with the Yanks whomping the Angels seven to nothing, but he wasn't. First batter, Murcer. The pitch! Way wide, ball one. Vick sank back down and stretched out on the carpet. Usually he'd grow tense, flex arms, shoulders, as if he himself were waiting for that fast ball, then swing, race for first. Or when the Yanks were in the field he'd make faces at the batter, call him shtunky names, dance when he struck out. Murcer walked. Vick yawned. Jerry Kenney came up next. Vick closed one eye, and Kenney became a blur—as far away as astronauts on the moon, and as misty and strange. It would be dumb, though, he decided, to turn off the set, because then Daf would be sure to start talking to him again.

Not that keeping it on would really stop her, though. What would? Nothing. Unless, maybe, he—ran away. Sure, get far away. So then she *couldn't* make him go with her tonight. Except, he'd promised. Only, he still didn't want to. So what if she was such a genius with her I.Q.! So how could he get away to some really great

place? Like Hawaii. Balancing on a surfboard, he'd coast
the waves forever. Then who'd care if Daddy moved out?
Or maybe go somewhere in baseball, a faraway stadium,
selling peanuts, and sleeping there too, in the dugout.
And then one morning they'd discover him, and ask
maybe if he knew how to be a bat boy.

"Vick?"

He started. Geez, why was she always sneaking?

She turned down the sound, about-faced and opened
her palm inches from his face.

"What do you think?"

"You got your hand so close, I can't see."

He watched her draw back, then saw she was cupping
a handful of subway tokens."

"So what's the big deal?"

"This way"—she snapped her fingers shut—"no bus
driver could remember us, or any of those change-booth
guys either."

I'm not going with you! He didn't say it, though.

"You see, uh"—he edged over to the set, and flicked the
sound back up—"well, this is a really tight game."

Seated at her play table, Daf absently ran a finger back
and forth over the pane of glass, while worriedly she
peered at the cutter, turning it on every side, almost as
if trying to figure out the meaning of each rivet holding it
together. What if this little black wheel thing wouldn't
work, like lots of times chemistry experiments didn't?
Or it broke? Or—if it did work now, and then it wouldn't
later, when they got there? When *they* . . . ? No, Vick
would come. He could never stand it if you called him a
liar or an Indian giver. Still, there was that time he hadn't

waited after school, and he'd promised. So . . . there had
to be other ways. Sure, like Sonny-James! Call him.
He'd be a lot better than Vick. And if Vick wouldn't
come, she'd just tell him to stay home by himself and bug
off!

Fiercely, tightly, clamping the glass against the table
with one hand, she began to draw the carbide blade
across it with the other. A grating, scratching noise got
made, about as loud as Mom's faraway tat-tat typing,
except the glass didn't seem to get cut. Was this thing
a fake? Maybe they'd sold her only a toy one. She tried
to picture Private Eye doing it. All she could remember,
though, was the glass splitting apart so easy, like slices of
cheese. She bent low, studying the scratch she'd made.
It was so faint. Rising, pressing down hard, with her
whole body, she rode the wheel across the ragged in-
dented line again. Now it looked deeper, and more
clear, but that's all. No real cutting. Still just a scratch.
Shit, it wasn't fair. The thing was supposed to be a *cutter*. And it was too late to go back and return it. They
were closed now, damn, damn, damn! Her fury subsiding,
she took another close look. Maybe—maybe you could
crack it along the scratch line, and that's how the gismo
was *supposed* to work. Gingerly she picked up one end
of the glass, the other end still resting on the wood, so
that it was diagonal to the table, and she pressed down
hard. Harder. Nothing. *Something* had to make it work.
Only what? Her eyes swept the bleak room. The putty
knife she used to scrape up modeling clay? Sure, she
could hammer down along the scratch with it. But where

was a hammer, hammer, hammer? She pulled off her shoe, placed the putty-knife blade against the glass, raised her arm, and doughtily swacked down. Crrrrrrckkkshhhh, the glass flew apart, slivers bouncing up and stinging her cheeks. Daf began to cry, silently.

Daphne dialed very slowly. Because what if Mom picked up the extension in her room? And what also took time was checking back to the card with that phone number on it after each digit. Finally, little beeps, and the ringing began. Suddenly she hung up. He'd say it was silly, or he'd be busy, practicing, or sleepy. Besides, who said *he* could work a glass cutter? Except—serial numbers. Glass cutters didn't have them, he'd said, and there *was* none anywhere on hers.

She tested the kitchen door to see if the chair she'd tucked under the knob still held firm. It seemed all right.

She dialed again.

"Hay-lo."

"It's me."

"No kiddin'."

"You're all busy tonight, aren't you?"

"Hunh? This is—*Who* did you say?"

"Don't you remember me?" What was the use? She felt like hanging up.

"Daphne?"

"Un-hunh." Joy spurted through her.

"Well. How you be?"

"Pretty good. How are you?"

"Oh, kickin' along pretty nice. What's into your haid? Feel like puttin' on some wheels with me again for tomorrow?"

"You all busy tonight?"

"You ain't allowed out at night, are ya?"

"Well, sometimes."

"Has to be tonight, hunh?"

"Well, sort of . . . I mean, you remember the stuff we talked about?"

"'Course I do. You mean—about your daddy?"

"Un-hunh."

"Ain't never gonna happen."

"You mean—you won't help me?"

"Help you what?"

"You know."

"Daf, whyn't I meet you tomorrow, like in the afternoon, five o'clock, say, front of your house. And then we'll just talk and talk, and then we gonna have us some real *good* stories. Okay?"

She hung up.

In the dark, hunched on a trunk in the hallway just outside her room, she strained to hear the noises which now and then were seeping through her parents' closed door. Earlier she'd heard Mom screech, "You bastard!" But now the voices were low, and the humming air conditioner in there wasn't helping any. This quiet stuff meant probably it was all settled now about his leaving.

She trembled, felt cold, and drew her pale-yellow sleepshirt, with the white lace down the front, more

closely about her. Her fingernail poked under a corner
of an old label pasted to the trunk. All the beach stuff
was in this one. Where in an apartment, Mom kept saying
and saying, are we going to find room for air mattresses?
Daf shut her eyes and imagined she was floating on
hers, way out past the breakers, to where the sky touches
the water. She'd come to a lighthouse. An old man with
a beard and hip boots would lead her up up the circular
stairs to the top. Seagulls would eat right out of her hand.
She'd be able to talk with them, bird talk. Then they'd
teach her how to fly, high, anywhere.

Her neck ached, her foot had fallen asleep, and still
all she could hear were mumbles. A thousand bees felt
like they were stinging her leg, as she lowered herself
and hobbled into her room. Before, while getting un-
dressed, she'd set her Donald Duck alarm for one o'clock.
She flicked on her pencil flash to recheck. Yup, still there,
and the lever still pulled out. Swinging the thin beam
about, she let it rest on her dresser, on her Orlon cardigan.
If she wrapped the clock in it, nobody would hear it
then but her. She wound the woollyish sweater about the
timepiece carefully, so the lever couldn't get pushed back
in by mistake. Having set the time-bomblike bundle under her bed, at the pillow end, she nipped out the flash
and snuggled in.

"Schaeffer is the one beer to have when you're having
more than one," crooned from a TV set somewhere across
the court, then galloping horses, gun shots. What if the
clock broke down and stopped? Crawling out, dropping
to the floor, she put her ear to the sweater. Mmmmmmm-
mmm. Damn, she'd half wished it *had* stopped.

Climbing back in, she heard a siren somewhere. Maybe an ambulance racing to the hospital, so the doctor could sew a girl back up before it was too late. A door snapped open, footsteps out in the hallway. Daddy, it had to be. She shut her eyes and waited. The footsteps kept coming, yes, softly, quietly, right into her room. They came close. Daddy would think she was sleeping. She felt his warm breath, lips on her forehead. In a second they were gone. That meant he was leaving, and he *couldn't* be.

"What did you and Mom decide?"

She watched him stop, turn, come back and take her hand.

"You mustn't worry."

"I know. But is that all?"

"For now, yes." He bent low and kissed her again. "Night, Daf."

"Stay with me?"

"I'm tired. Some other night. Tomorrow maybe."

She waited for the door to close, then slammed her head against the headboard. It hurt bad, even inside her teeth.

In her dream she was under water picking flowers, even bigger ones than the Museum of Natural History exhibit, and she wasn't afraid of the prehistoric octopus either, because her air mattress was faster than any submarine, and she had a ray gun too. But something down below was ringing, ringing, ringing. Except she was all dry, and in bed, and it was the alarm. She tumbled to the floor, fumbled with the sweater, and got the lever pushed in. Though in her head she could still hear the ringing.

Could Dad or Mom have heard? Supercarefully she opened her door a crack and listened. A truck rumbled somewhere, or a bus, but that was all. She edged out and into Vick's room. For a second she chewed on her thumbnail, then tapped his shoulder.

He rolled away on his side.

"Vick," she whispered, then tried tickling under his chin. She saw his eyes open. "Come on. We got to go now."

She waited while blearily he hoisted himself up, and then seemed to fall asleep again, sitting.

"You going to get dressed?"

He shrugged, but then swung his legs out, resignedly.

Back in her room Daf speedily pulled on her dungarees, tied sneaker laces, buckled the straps on her schoolbag, yanked it up off the chair, and tiptoed out.

At the front door, undoing the locks, she froze. Pung-pung-click, what a racket! She'd never realized how loud those tumblers were. Mom could come rushing out. Or Daddy. Both. Where were they? Vick right behind her was breathing almost as loud as those dumb locks. She turned back to him.

"You got everything? Sun glasses?"

He tapped his breast pocket and nodded.

"Gloves?"

Into his hip pocket he reached, exhumed a pair, and dangled them in front of her.

Daf smiled. He was on the ball, more than, but then . . . "Hey, where's your hat?"

"Come on, will you?" he whined, and tried to push past her.

146

"Next to fingerprints"—she stopped him—"hairs are the most giveaway clues."

"Will you stop it?"

"Why do you think in restaurants the cooks all wear hats?"

"Boy, oh boy!" But he turned and slouched back toward his room.

Going out, he wore his NYY (for New York Yankees) cap. Her head was covered with a white pompom-topped beret.

At the top of the steps descending into the subway, again she stopped him.

"Now what?"

"Just remember, don't ever turn and face the change booth."

"What if he remembers my cap?"

"Very funny."

As soon as they'd pushed through the heavy turnstiles, she grabbed his hand and hurried him along the bleak platform, so the change-maker shouldn't remember even their backs.

"There's a cop," he suddenly whispered.

"Where?"

He pointed with his chin to the far end of the platform.

"Pretend we don't even care."

Daf faced the wall and stared hard at the poster, a picture of a happy Black Man: "Assistant Sportswear Buyer, I got my job through THE NEW YORK TIMES."

"I hate that newspaper."

Vick didn't answer.

"Every other paper has funnies except that one."

147

He moved away and sat on the bench.

She didn't like the way he was being so quiet and never looking at her. "What's the matter?"

"You know, we might end up roasting in hell."

"Oh that hell stuff is only for Catholics."

"You think, no matter what you do, there's no God to punish you?"

"I asked Miss Kornzweig once about dead things. They just get eaten up by worms and bugs in the ground. And all you do is turn into dirt, and then . . ."

The roaring train arrived, drowning out the argument.

Quiet for a moment while they boarded, and then the train noise grew loud, deafening, howling, an Apollo blast-off, louder than Daf ever remembered it, a million people screaming, falling from the Empire State. It hurt. She put hands over her ears.

At the Times Square station everyone was Black, and staring at them. Avoiding them, her eyes fixed down on the grimy concrete, tightly she clutched Vick's hand, while hurriedly they climbed upward. Only three steps left, she tilted her head back to see the ceiling. That trail of little overhead green lights, which led you to the crosstown shuttle train, where was it?

"I'm hungry." Vick's elbow was waggling toward a frozen-custard/hotdog stand.

"Shhhhhhh, there they are!" She'd spotted the glowing green markers finally, and tugged him forward.

"We got money."

"Yeah, but the guy would have to hear our voices."

On the uptown side she eyed the mirror over a gum machine. No one really near it. She sauntered very casually up to it. How great! With these sun glasses, no one in a million years could know it was her. She adjusted her beret, tilting it just a little.

"You know, they ought to have a kid with them on *International Secret Mission*."

"Yeah, sure, a girl."

When was Vick going to stop being so sour and mean?

This train was bright, glaring, right through her shades even. It was empty, though. And more quiet.

Vick was trying hard not to think about anything but the subway map, and keeping track of the two stops till they were supposed to get off, but it still all felt wrong. But could he ever get her to change her mind any more? How? She was so positive. Anything he said, she'd bounce it back twice as hard. So the best maybe would be to go with it for keeps, once and for all stop trying, arguing. More words, though, began yipping out anyway.

"Why would smart big shots, like rabbis and President Nixon, pray all the time if God wasn't real?"

"Did you ever see him?"

"You can't see a lot of things."

"Name one."

"Germs."

Daf looked up at an ad, a lady in a bikini, exhaling smoke, Virginia Slims, smiling. *She* sure wasn't worrying about germs.

"Well, if that stuff about your soul living on and on forever is true, everything's okay. 'Cause after we get rid of that Mrs. Nyland, she'll just come right back again and be somebody else."

What if, Vick wondered, she really could?

CHAPTER 15

"Next corner, Sonny. Take a left."

"I know."

Shut your fool dumb-ass mouth! Shit, di'nt she know, every damn bit of talkin' she did now hurt—bright as a whip woman like Ray?

But then, making the turn, his lips began to curl, a brief flicker, hidden by his beard. Still, it was a smile. Hell, all that cramped-stomach longing, anxious teeth-grinding, circling, circling that phone like forever, prayin' she'd call back. Now she never would. Definite. Sure. He felt light, easy, like a load hoisted off his chest so he could breathe, off the top of his head too. All that over, finished, could it be—while taking one swing of the wheel? He inhaled deeply. Cruddy New York City air smelled okay.

He spotted a parking space just beyond her doorway, and pulled up to it.

"Just double park, and I'll hop out."

"Hell, take me a second."

Easily he maneuvered into it.

Rachel immediately sprung open the tricky door, and ducked out onto the sidewalk.

"Bye Sonny. And good luck."

Her heels click-clicked quickly away. He watched the old red-nosed doorman swing open the door, saw it close. Darkness all around, except for the pool of light at the deserted portal. His fingers drummed on the dashboard. The kid, the cute child, Daphne, if he'd told Ray about her, would *that* have made a difference? "Rachel, you go on gettin' in deep with this lawyer man, and you gonna meet a sweet little girl who hates you. Fact, she's even talkin' about killin' you." 'Cept Ray probably would have just walked away, with contempt, thinkin' he'd made it up—too fantastic. Weird coincidence, though, what with tonight bein' Daphne's big dream night.

He sat back, lit a cigarillo. Now where to?

Climbing from the lit subway stairs into the darkness above, Daphne's tummy tightened. A look up Lexington, though, and she felt better. The street lights were nicely spaced out, like guards, and bright. The only thing that might be really scary were the black recessed store entrances, where you could never know if anyone was hiding unless you got right up close. But then you didn't have to, 'cause there was hardly any traffic, and you could go out into the street and slide along next to the parked cars.

She felt Vick take her hand.

"We better go together."

His warm palm felt good, but she wrenched free.

"Separate. You agreed."

"Yeah, but it's awful late."

"Separate they never spot you so easy. Geez, last night you saw how Private Eye did it."

"You know"—Vick was shaking his head—"you're not allowed alone. Daddy'd get mad as hell. And he'd blame me."

Suddenly her schoolbag arm curled back, she swung, swatting him meanly. "Just 'cause you're bigger doesn't mean *you're* the boss."

Stunned, he rubbed his arm and shoulder.

She scuttled away without looking back. At the corner, though, she sneaked a backward glance. Yeah, he was following.

Mrs. Nyland's street was darker, but more sleepy-looking than creepy really. Daf began counting the windows with lights in them. Seven, eight . . . and then strain for a glimpse of Vick darting along on the opposite side. He'd disappear, and she'd all but stop breathing. She'd peer ahead to a gap between parked cars, where a hydrant was, and finally he'd flit past.

What if they could never get in? Because what if everyone who lived in that building had gone to bed already, so the doorman would never go up in the elevator, and they could never get past him? She yawned. Well, then they could go back to bed too.

The entrance was getting real close now. Daf stopped, counted, six more windows, then the door. She edged down off the sidewalk, slipped between two parked cars, then inched ahead closer, hugging herself against the cars. After a monster shiny Cadillac, there were two motorcycles. Yeah, they'd be perfect. Easy to peek over, and see through, and still hide behind. She waved to Vick, but where was he? The fourth time he finally scooted over.

153

"D'you see that?"

"What?"

Vick pointed with his thumb. "His car."

Beyond the big bikes, all she could see was just a plain ordinary car. "Whose?"

"Your cowboy's."

To see what he was talking about, she snuck out toward the middle of the street.

God, it was Sonny-James'—or one just like his. Only in the dark it looked more like a giant hotdog. Warily, crouching still, she moved closer to it. Yeah, it was his all right. Glimmering faintly, hints of purplish pink, enough though so it *had* to be his. But—why? Unless—unless, what if he'd *told* her, and now he was up there guarding her? But—but why should he be? She inched along the side, until at the door she rose, slowly. Suddenly she dropped to the asphalt. Trembling. Had that been him in there? She wanted to race back to Vick, ached to. She *had* to know, though. Again she rose, forcing herself really to look this time. A head lolled back on the top of the seat. Him, yes. But sleeping. But here?

Vick was stretched out between the motorcycles when she got back.

"Lots of other people could have the same kind of car, you know."

She stretched out next to him. They waited. Car lights, getting closer, brighter, spreading everywhere, blinding. She tried to melt into the street. A door slammed, the lights went away. Daf saw a lady go in, wobbling on high heels, yes, the fat one in tight yellow pants who'd

154

given Sonny-James the bawling out. Only now she was in a tent dress. The front door closed after her.

"One hundred," Daf murmured tensely, "two hundred, three hundred, four hundred," then poked her brother, sprang up, and lunged forward, the schoolbag slapping against her thigh as she ran. The doorknob, though, would not turn. She pulled, pushed, leaned into it with all her might. Tears started to come.

"It was never locked. Never."

"We were never here at night."

"Vick, watch out. We're right in the light." She gave his sleeve a sharp tug and rushed back to their hiding place.

He hurried after her.

Stretching out on his stomach, he sighed, "Well, maybe there is a God. And this shows he don't want us to."

"He does too!" 'Cause Sonny-James is sleeping! But she didn't want Vick to know about that. "'Cause we got all the tools—and everything."

Vick shrugged, and tried to find a comfortable spot on the tire to rest his head. A couple more minutes probably, and she'd be ready to head back home. He heard her making noises, though, monkeying with something. What in the world else could she try? He raised his head and saw her unstrapping the schoolbag, feeling around in it for something. Why? Hell, what was the difference? Besides, he didn't feel like talking to her.

Again a car, blinding lights, coins tinkling, a taxi getting paid and zooming off. Two people went in this time. Vick heard his sister counting once more. Four hundred, five hundred, and abruptly she thrust her bag at him, and went hurtling off—but by herself.

Maybe, she prayed, if she ran fast enough, the lock wouldn't have snapped shut yet. Shit, no, it had. And again the knob wouldn't turn, not even budge. So—so this had to be the only way. She pressed the blade of her cutter against the extreme outer edge of the glass, the pane just below the knob. Should she go ahead, cut? But the noise, the grating, people would hear, call the police. Hell, let them! She tightened her grip and pushed down, hard. Zzzzzzzp, zzzzzzzzp, zzzzzzzzp, zzzzzzzzp, four solid strokes, one for each side of the oblong perimeter. But nothing happened, just like at home. The glass was still in place. She placed her palm against it and pushed. Harder, with all her might. Still nothing. She glanced backward. Was Vick laughing? Too dark, she couldn't see. And any second the doorman would be back. There had to be *some* way. A kick? She gripped the knob with both hands, raised a foot, planted her left sole against the pane, pulled it back, and kicked violently. Suddenly she pitched forward, banging her face against the door. Pain flamed through her face and head.

That same second, it seemed, Vick was there, helping lift her back out. Her foot had gone clear through, so that she'd been straddling the door.

"You all right?"

She nodded. If she opened her mouth, she might cry out loud.

"You are something."

She put a finger to her lips, then to his.

Vick froze, and then heard what she'd heard, the elevator, creaking to a halt, probably its door opening now. Fast, deftly, he reached in, snatched the piece of glass up off the rubber mat, and pushed her back ahead of him to their motorcycles.

"Fantastic." Carefully he examined the pane. "This thing's still all in one piece."

"See. God does want us to."

Could that really be, he wondered? God did kill people, like when he drowned the Egyptian Army. But that was so long ago . . . "What happens when the doorman discovers this is missing?"

"I don't know . . . Maybe he won't."

They waited. Vick curled up against his tire. Daf kept watch. Maybe the old doorkeeper wouldn't come out again, 'cause no one else might come, all night, and it never would be discovered. But then, how would they ever get in? . . . Suddenly a figure was standing out on the sidewalk, looking up at the sky, to see like if it was going to rain—the doorman! He went back in, and never did seem to notice. She started to poke her brother, but stopped. Let him sleep till it's time.

After a while Daf looked at her watch, but couldn't quite make it out. But maybe that was good, 'cause if it was getting light, Mom might find they were gone, and then she'd call the whole police to come out looking for them. And—what if they were caught? Handcuffs too. Well, Daf would tell the cops it was all her fault. So at least Vickie would stay free.

Car lights again. Now, maybe, finally. Shit, it wasn't even slowing. As it passed, she spotted the unlit searchlight on top. The two cops inside were all busy talking to each other.

Then, like a minute later, she heard footsteps, strong ones, no high heels. Could that be Sonny-James maybe? Except it was the other direction. Raising her eyes a hair above the motorcycle seat, she saw the silhouette of a man, very tall, heading right for the door. He came into the light and stopped, waiting for the doorman.

She began prodding Vick with her fingers, knuckles, fists. A split second after the man had gone in, they were both just outside the thick door, crouching, listening. Had the man noticed the pane was missing? Was he telling? But they heard no talking, only the elevator slamming shut. Vick reached in through the oblong hole, and turned the knob. They streaked across the lobby and slipped into the stairwell.

Cracks of gunshots, hotness creasing his temple and cheeks, bullets whistling past inches away, Sonny-James was falling, landing hard, painfully, on jagged rocks. Sharpshooters, up in the hills, they'd ambushed him, shot his poor sweet horse right out from under him, Injuns, or was it little girls with long dark hair? Except this wasn't some dumb-ass John Wayne nightmare. His foot really did hurt. He shook himself and unstuck his eyes. What in—was he still here in the car? Why? With his foot all bent up and snaked under the hand brake. And a crick in his neck too.

He untwisted his gone-to-sleep foot, dragged himself out of the car, and stood, letting the blood circulate back in. Then, limping at first, he ambled up the street. Just around the corner on York Avenue, he recalled a bar that might still be open. Get some of that dryness and sour taste out. Maybe wash away some of that dream too.

Yeah, what in hell was a child doing, shooting a rifle at him? What in hell was some little girl doing, shooting a rifle at anybody, and so dang expertly too?

The beer, instead of smoothing away all those sharpnesses, though, seemed to make him feel even more itchy, funny, unsettled. He ordered more.

This Daphne kid, what if she really was trying to kill Rachel? Bull. How could she? Couldn't make it with no gun, that's for sure. Explode a bomb? Poison? Gas? He chuckled to himself. Each new notion got more way out than the last. But then her cute-tense voice on the phone, why was it echoing inside his head? "You mean you won't help me?" "Help you what?" he'd answered. "*You* know," she'd said so flatly, tiny-sounding, helpless almost, and yet down under that cutesy kid stuff, there'd been something hard, electric, like it really would push and push, no matter what.

Hell, why sweat it?

Rachel, in her nightgown, about to turn in, was adjusting her window air conditioner when the phone rang. She positioned the master control knob on lo cool. It wasn't at all hot really, but the constant throb would at least mute out the more grating street noises.

"That you, Rachel?"

"Yes."

"You okay? Just wanted to be sure."

"I'm okay. Thanks. Goodnight."

She flicked off the lamp and snuggled under. She'd

been tempted to ask, *Why* this strange call? But that surely would have led to a conversation.

Sonny-James, crossing back over to his stool, beckoned to the bartender for another beer, *and* a double bourbon. Dang, he didn't feel any easier than before.

CHAPTER 16

The door from the basement out to the courtyard was locked tight. Why had she listened to him? She'd known coming down here would be a waste. The roof was the only way. Except, well, who really wanted to go all the way up there?

"So why don't you cut this glass too?"

"Look." Daphne pointed.

On the outside, a wire grate webbed it over. Breaking wouldn't do any good. Besides, even in this faint light Vick could see the bottom rung of the fire escape was way too high. Daf, even standing on his shoulders, could never reach.

Daf, tilting her head back and gazing up at the black window squares, lined straight up to the roof and then the moon, suddenly imagined herself walking right up the side of the building in suction shoes, like a circus tight-rope girl. Sharper than Private Eye even. But, what if the suction broke down, like a flat tire, and you fell?

The stairs felt like forever, climbing, climbing, till like maybe finally you were at the end, but there were more, always more, like there had to be more stairs here than the Statue of Liberty, or the Empire State, or the two together. The World Trade Center, somebody had said, didn't have stairs. Only elevators. Pulling on banister rails, hands sweating inside gloves, legs aching, collapsing at landings, panting, catching one another as they faltered, Daf and Vick lurched upward.

Vick, pushing open a door to coolness, a breeze, at last, the soft glowy darkness of the roof, sprawled out on his back. Maybe she'd let him sleep a minute.

"You wait right here."

He swung his head around and watched her move off. God, she was still lugging that heavy schoolbag carefully as ever too. Where'd she get the strength? Fantastic. Quickly she reached the edge. Then she was sort of marching-pacing, first in one direction, about-face the other way, then to the side. What in heck was she . . . ? Oh yeah, sure, like she was getting out of the elevator, pretending, like arriving at Mrs. Nyland's, so she could be sure which fire escape was the right one. Now her free hand was in the air, motioning to him, waving he should come over. He felt like pretending he really *was* asleep.

At the brink she bent to retie her shoelaces, then remained crouching and redid his too. Everything tonight was weird, but her tying a double bow on his sneakers —that made his throat clog.

She stood up. "Okay?" she asked.

He shrugged.

"You ready, or aren't you?"

"I don't know if I can."

"Sure you can," and she punched his shoulder.

Step after step, suddenly he *was* moving, downward, away from the hazy warmth of the roof, deeper and deeper into darkness. Daphne, inches behind, echoed his every gesture and movement, a slight, graceful shadow. About the courtyard, air conditioners hummed and buzzed, comfortingly helping dim their treads, rustling of sleeves against bodies, and the tip-tap flip-flops of their shoelaces. The TV sounds were nice too, mostly snatches from an open window somewhere below, had to be a late late movie, a man and woman cooing, "Darling, I love you. Mmmmmm," with violins playing soft and then loud. If only, only, Daf yearned, the noises she and Vick were making could sound like just a few more violins. A faraway cat screeched. Daf froze. Had that animal seen them? Smelled them? Could it be trying to warn people, like a watchdog? She held her breath, waiting for more screeches. Finally, she had to let it out.

Halfway down the next step, Vick stopped. So abruptly that Daf's knee pummeled accidentally into his rear.

"Sorry."

"That's okay."

"Why'd you stop?"

"Smell."

She did. Geez, something did smell a little queer. Sweet and sour sort of.

"Okay. So what?"

"Geraniums."

A few steps up from the landing he began to see them too, and not just geraniums, but all kinds of plants, everywhere, small pots, large planters—a jungle. How could you ever get through?

"We'll have to go back."

"You crazy?"

163

"Look."

"But they're just—plants."

"You'd have to step all over them."

"Who cares?"

"They'd crash. Wake up the whole world. Besides, you want us to kill plants too?"

"Well—well couldn't we just pick some up—on top of the others?"

Yeah, he thought, you could probably, the small ones, enough to make a little path. Only who wanted to?

"Well," she demanded, "come on."

Then she bent and began. He sighed, and joined her, lifting the pots while she took up the under-dishes. A slippery oval shape, though, with a huge spreading snake plant in it, wouldn't balance. Vick had to lay it on its side. Dirt dribbled out, grating slightly falling between the slats, splattering louder and louder from landing to landing, then crackling like gunshots as it plopped down on the concrete court. Vick wanted to flatten himself against the slats, hide. No room, though. He couldn't turn and race back either, with Daf square in his way. He shut his eyes. That TV was still going. "Oh, how I do love you." Violins. "Yes, this night must never end." More violins. Where were the angry screams, searchlights, police whistles?

He'd reached almost where the stairs began again, but now leaves were everywhere, up over his head even. A rubber tree had branches across the whole width of the fire escape. You'd never get past it. They'd *have* to go back. Suddenly the biggest branch was moving. Daf had grabbed it, was bending it away, and so easily.

Daf was counting now, step by step. Four more, and they'd be there, her floor. At the next-to-last step, she reached and clutched at Vick's sweatshirt. He turned. She pointed her forefinger decisively back and forth at the window directly ahead of them.

"You sure?"

She nodded and then pointed to their right, to a window with a buzzing-brrrrrng air conditioner in it.

"Her bedroom. This here's the kitchen."

Vick, staring ahead at the closed black window, felt a pain in his leg, his ankle, sharp claws piercing into him. On the floor, just inside, she might have a bear trap.

Daf moved ahead, leaving him on the bottom step, while she crept over to the window. Almost instantly, it seemed to him, she drew out her cutter, pressed it against the glass, and like a machine almost, rolled its wheel up, across, down and across. Then she laid her hand flat against the pane, about to push.

He couldn't let her. "Wait." He grabbed her arm.

For a second she didn't budge or say a word. Then without turning, she hissed through her teeth, "Wait for what?"

Vick tried to think of something. Only, what?

She pushed. Immediately the glass fell in, shattering, tinkling, crashing. A million people *had* to hear. Daf burrowed herself against the few inches of wall below the window, held her breath, and died, and died again. The air conditioner didn't stop rumbling, though, and the TV violins kept playing. Only now there were guitars with them too.

Vick, who'd curled up against the outside rail, positive that any second it had to be all over, heard new little rustlings. He opened his eyes. Could she *still* be going ahead? He saw his sister shaking a can, poking her arm inside the window. He inched toward her, shimmying on his belly. She was spraying an aerosol on the window locks, and around the sides.

He murmured into her ear, "What's that?"

"So it'll slide easier."

And then she *was* unscrewing the lock. Like it was the easiest thing. She motioned to him to lift the window. Warily he applied both palms to the underside of the frame, lifted, and it did rise, smoothly.

Sonny-James wished he'd brought along a set of earplugs. Bars, Lord knows, were meant for talkin', but both sides of him guys were yip-yappin' about craziness, and not lettin' up or slowin' down neither. He looked up at the clock: two forty-five. One hell of a time for a debate about demagnetizers. Made him a little mad too, not havin' the foggiest what demagnetizers even were, till one of 'em finally threw in somethin' about Sony tape recorders, which still didn't really explain it. Two faggots to the other side were goin' on about double overhead cam engines in Ghiblis, displacements in Lamborghinis, twin chokes, carburetor ductings. He got up, took his beer, and veered away to an empty booth just opposite. Insane, all-out bughouse, people talkin' about, dreamin' about nothin' but machines; demagnetizers, displacements . . . guns. Was that screwed-up little girl with her guns and her killin' gonna start yammerin' inside his head again?

To get her away, he conjured up the log cabin in the Smokies, nestled into the side of Goose Mountain, three miles of sweet-smellin' pines to the nearest human bein'. No Sonys, twin chokes, or homicidal kids anywheres around. So what in Christ was he doin' stayin', settin' in this New York bar?

Next second he was in the phone booth. Talk to the child, get it cleared away, or he'd never get out of this freaked-out city.

Henry shot bolt upright, startled, but not really wholly awake. So dark, and the alarm already? And so loudly. But only in spasms. So it had to be the phone. Now?

He groped for it, finally got it between his fingers, to his ear.

"Hello. Yes?"

"Say, uh, is Daphne at home?"

"Daphne?"

"Un-hunh, Daphne Beckman, she there? Could I speak to her?"

"Who is this?"

"You her daddy?"

"Yes."

"Could you jes do me a *big* favor, and go check if she's in her bed?"

"What are you? What is this?"

"See, I'm kind of a friend, and I'm, you know, worried about her—bein' out, that's all."

"You haven't done somethin' to her, have you?"

"No, no, no, no. See, she was talkin' 'bout goin' out and killin' someone tonight, and I'd sure feel easier if I knew for sure she'd stayed home."

"Mister, I don't know what kind of a nut you are, but you ought to find yourself a good headshrinker, and fast." Henry slammed down the receiver.

"Did we actually get a dirty phone call?" Joanne asked drowsily.

"Yeah."

Henry's head hurt as he lay back down. Who? Who could that have been? And why? Who could hate him so? And be so vicious as to use Daphne?

The phone, ringing, again.

"Who are you, you bastard? What do you want?"

"Did ya check? She there, or she gone out?"

"You trying to blackmail me, threaten me? What *is* this?"

"Mister, like I said, I'm jes worried about that little girl. And I would sure be a lot less tensed up if you went and took a look, and *told* me she was safe in her bed."

Henry for a long second held the receiver away from his ear, as if it didn't really exist, as if it were some incredible apparition that in a moment would vanish. Then abruptly he let it drop on the mattress, slid out of bed, and hurried to Daphne's room.

In seconds he was back.

"What *is* this?" The ferocity in his voice had changed to breathless terror. "Do you want money? Where *is* she?"

Henry waited. It seemed hours. The voice at the other end was breathing but not answering.

168

"I don' know where she is either. But she was talkin' about goin' out and killin' Rachel."

Daphne had lowered one foot in through the window and now was carefully swinging in the other.

"Wait a second," Vick murmured from within.

Daf stopped. Shining her pencil flash around the walls, she couldn't find him. Finally she picked him out just under the window, bent over the floor with a brush and dustpan, sweeping up the broken glass.

"What's that for?"

"So nobody'll get cut."

Boy. And he thought *she* did nutty things.

Stepping lightly down, Daphne squeezed past him to the stove, where she put down her schoolbag and tucked her fingers under the ends of the burner plate. Gently, oh so delicately, she lifted it, lowered her head to the flame and blew out the pilot. Then she knelt and began unpacking the Saran, funnel, tubing, tape. Suddenly she rose, crept to him, and whispered, "D'you check her bedroom, if it was closed?"

"Has to be"—he shrugged—"She's got the air conditioning."

Boy, could he be a lazy good-for-nothing. He could *at least* have gone to look, to be sure. Probably, though, he was right, or Mrs. Nyland would have heard the glass break and screamed—and caught them.

"Hold the light for me."

He shone it for her on the open oven while she applied the tape, making only one really bad stick-em-together mistake, where she had to throw away a piece and start over. Quickly, really, she had the funnel in place and then the Saran. She'd just begun fitting the tubing onto and around the funnel, when suddenly the light was gone. She turned and saw Vick at the refrigerator, taking out something, then biting into it.

"You still need light?" he asked.

"That all you can do, eat?"

"Only one peach."

"If you're not doing the light, at least you're supposed to be on lookout."

He padded over to the door, peered out into the dark hall, and shrugged.

Daphne, her apparatus all connected, felt around the edges to make sure none of the tape was curling off, and then started to unroll the tubing, crawling along the linoleum past the sink cabinets, snaking it past Vickie at the doorway, on into the hallway along the carpeting, past the bathroom, until . . .

Her door, open? A crack, it was! Suddenly Daf's fingers became numb. The tubing slipped away. Had Mrs. Nyland heard? Been listening all the time? Unless—what if she weren't in there, weren't even home? So look and see. Did she dare? Daf bit down on her lip, slowly raised her head, and tried to peep in. Too dark. And anyway the bed was way over on the other side. The air conditioning, though, was rumbling and groaning on like perfectly normal. And it wouldn't be doing that, would it, if no one were home? Daf reached back along the rug for the tubing, and gingerly fed it in through the sliver-like opening, further and further until there was no more slack.

Back in the kitchen, standing before the stove, she

placed her fingers over the oven knob. "Okay put your hand," she gently commanded, "on top of mine."

"What for?"

"So we do it together."

Where was Vick? Suddenly she couldn't see him. Then he was framed in the window, clambering out. Her mouth opened for a yell, a curse. But what was the use?

She turned back to the stove, stared at it hard for a second, or an hour, then closed her eyes, tightened her fingers on the knob, and turned it, slowly, all the way. She stood stock-still, waiting. Would God strike her dead now? Nothing happened, though.

Edging back toward the window, she moved sideways. She couldn't stop staring back at the stove somehow, listening to its low hiss, even while she was climbing out.

CHAPTER 17

Her heart pounding, eyes tearing, smarting, Daf was stepping down off the topmost fire-escape platform onto the roof, the solid roof. And she was positive, trying with all her might to feel positive, Vick would be right there waiting for her. He *had* to be. But where? He couldn't have left, he couldn't have. Maybe inside, in the stairwell. She hurried over to the black mass sitting on the middle of the roof, and grabbed the gritty, rusty doorknob.

"It's locked."

Vick! God, she hated him. But still she was so glad to see him too. He sat a few feet off, hunched against the brick wall.

"You mean, we're stuck up here?"

"I don't even care."

"Well, nothing happened. I mean, about God striking me."

"You feel bad about her?"

"You mad at me?"

"No. Just scared."

She lowered herself next to him. "You think there's really a place where elephants pick you up with their trunks, and they have live princesses?"

173

"Sure. Siam." He patted her.

Noises, footsteps, lots of them, coming up inside the stairwell, closer, louder, then the door groaning open. One, two, three shapes, men, came out, inches away. She could almost touch the legs of one of them. They looked off toward the fire escapes, lit up powerful flashlights, began sweeping the roof with them.

"Naaah, there's no one here."

"Nine years old, that what you said?"

"Officer, you saw that there front door, di'nt you?"

"Fella, how do I know *you* didn't cut out that glass?"

But they did start walking off toward the edge. Only it didn't help. The gnawing in Daf's stomach hurt just as much. Would they be caught? No, please. Fink, Sonny-James. *All* cowboys! Just as phony as all grownups.

"Should we warn them?" Vick whispered. "Maybe they can still save her."

"Artificial respiration?"

"Yeah."

"Vick, in reform school, you think they'd let us stay together?"

"No. It'd be like camp. You have to eat with your own group."

Vick suddenly leaped up, and was running toward the flashlights.

Faraway something was ringing. Ringing and ringing, but it was so hard for Rachel to open her eyes, to move. The phone? Middle of the night? Wrong number.

Or some crank. Why didn't they stop? Nnnnnnnn. Nnnnnnnnn. The air conditioner, thank God, softened it a little. Nnnnnnnnnnn. Nnnnnnnnnn. Some relation could have died. Funny smell, damn smog. She groped for the receiver, got it to her ear, but upside down, had to drop it before she could get it the right way.

"Ray, that you? You all right?"

"Henry, what's the matter?"

"Look, uh, I don't know how to tell you this, but my kids are missing."

"What?"

"I just got this grotesque phone call. He claims Daphne said something about killing you tonight."

". . . You can't be serious."

"Nothing unusual's happened over there?"

"No. Does Joanne know?"

"I let her think it was a dirty phone call. I'm in the kitchen now."

"You going to call the police?"

"I don't know."

"Wait a second, will you, Henry? Something's funny here."

She fumbled for the lamp switch, found it, hid her eyes a second from the glare, and then lowered her feet to the rug. Her nose crinkled. Why'd it smell so queer? At the door, she felt something under her bare sole. She bent. Rubber shower tubing? Why?

She flicked on the kitchen light and saw the weird childlike contraption. Rachel screamed, loudly, uncontrollably. Her lungs and throat gave out, and still she screamed, inaudibly.

Handcuffs, after you got used to them, Daf decided, didn't feel all that terrible—as long as the person you were chained to didn't yank too much. Vick's eyes were closed, so she couldn't tell if he was sleeping or worried or still mad at her. It was so quiet now. Why had the talking all stopped? Mrs. Nyland was still reading the paper the policeman had been writing on. The two cops were just watching. Weren't they ever going to let Sonny-James back in? What had *he* done wrong? Or maybe he'd escaped. Then her eyes closed.

She was stepping between the daffodils, then burrowing through the hedge to Gloria's. Police sirens screaming, coming closer, but Gloria, all ready, was reaching through the hedge and taking her hand.

"Daf, you moving back here now?"

"No, I just escaped from reform school. I need a hideout."

"You can hide in here. Look." Gloria pulled on some grass, and a tiny sod door rose up from the lawn. It led underground.

Down the steps in the secret room was a whole Barton's candy counter, and a make-believe inside of a house, with a whole doll family living in it, doll furniture, a baby doll with a crib, a pet dog doll, a rifle for the little boy doll. But machines were making noises, real machines, a washer and a dryer both, whirring away in a corner.

"What're those doing in here?"

"Look." Gloria pointed to the washer's glass door.

Mommy? Daf saw a face, soapy water splashing over it, and then her mother was spinning, upside down, faster and faster, now pounding—bang, bang, bang, bang, "Let me out!" Daf turned away to the dryer, and saw another face through the glass. Daddy, with a pair of socks stuffed in his mouth, so he couldn't even yell.

Gloria was giggling.

"No," Daphne said firmly, "they have to stay in there. I'm not even allowed to *touch* those machines."

Was someone shaking her hand? Why did her wrist hurt? Something digging into it. Daf woke, saw the handcuffs. Vick was shifting position, raising his legs up onto the couch.

"I prefer not to sign this," Mrs. Nyland told the policeman.

"Lady, if that's not exactly what you said, gimme corrections."

"I'm sorry. I'm not signing anything. Not without a lawyer."

The door buzzed. The other officer went to open. Someone new coming in. Daf snapped shut her eyes. Daddy. He hated her now. Forever. She couldn't hear really the soft things he was saying to Mrs. Nyland, sounded like kisses even, maybe. So what! Daf would just keep her eyes shut. She'd never see him again. Except maybe at reform school, visiting day. But she'd tell him not to come.

Her wrists were hurting again, rough hands squeezing her. Then she felt the handcuffs slip off.

"Daphne, open your eyes."

She saw the policemen were going out. Daddy's face and eyes looked so red, like he'd been crying.

"Come," he said.

"You mean we're not arrested?"

"No."

She couldn't figure this out. "Why not?"

"Because . . ." Henry choked.

Mrs. Nyland spoke. "Because you didn't *really* know what you were doing."

Like fish! Daf didn't say it out loud, though.

Out in the hall, waiting for the elevator, Daf looked back and saw Sonny-James, crouched in a corner by Mrs. Nyland's door. Funny. Who cared, though?

The street felt chilly. Daddy kept looking for a taxi. They walked slowly.

Nothing, Daf decided, ever happened how it was supposed to. 'Cause if they weren't getting sent to reform school, what *would* happen? "So," she asked finally, "when are you going to marry her?"

"Soon, I think. Rachel did a beautiful thing, you know, not accusing you."

"Maybe someday," Vick mused, "after five years, she'll like us."

"I don't even care." Daf meant it too.

"Kids, would you like to go away with me for a bit? Just the three of us. Out to Block Island maybe, and we'll just try and talk and talk—about everything."

"You think that'll do any good?"

"Yes." Henry squeezed her to him.

At the corner she looked back. The sun, a fiery rim, was just peeking up over the river. What if maybe God *had* been watching all night long?